Another Cypress Sky
By Kenneth Thomas

Another Cypress Sky

Beneath Cypress Skies, Volume 2

Kenneth Thomas

Published by Kenneth Thomas, 2024.

ANOTHER CYPRESS SKY

First edition. December 26, 2024.

ISBN: 979-8230406549

Written by Kenneth Thomas.

Also by Kenneth Thomas

Alchemists Cost
Eternity's Past

Beneath Cypress Skies
Another Cypress Sky

Harrow Harbor Mysteries
Whispering Harbor Mystery
The Secret of the Cavern
The Ghost Ships Shadow

Moonlight Pact series
The Moonlight Pact
The Rift Redemption
The Riftbound Legacy

The Awakening Thread Chronicles
The Awakening Thread

The Broke Kids Club
The Broke Kids Club
The Broke Kids Club: Ripples of Change

The Broke Kids Club Collection
The Broke Kids Club Collection

The Convergence of Minds series
The Digital Agora: A Philosophical Epic of AI and Humanity
Foundation of the Agora
Beyond the Agora: Fractured Realms

The Echoes of Eternity
The Awakening of Nephira
The Rift Of Worlds

The Eclipse Chronicles

Shards of Light
Eclipse Reaver
Axis Reforged

The Veil of Shadows Series
Shattered Dominion
The Fractured Path

Standalone
A Tail of Darkness To Light
The Mirror Within
Echoes of Ink and Heart
Purpose Over Power: The Visionary Path of Servant
Leadership
The Questions That Shape Us: Finding Life's Wisdom-The
Power of Inquiry
Where the Shadows Settle
30 Days to Inner Freedom: A Mindful Journey in Addiction
Recovery
Towards a Sustainable Future: The UN's 17 Goals
Echoes of Becoming
Cognitive Freedom: The Stoic Path to Resilience and
Recovery
Beneath the Cypress Sky
The Unbroken Pen
Where Tides Meet
Whispers on Petals

A Love Written In Starlight
The Twilight Alchemy of Jekyll and Hyde
Whispers of the Wild Frontier
The Last Prediction
Tales of the Midnight Traveler
Echoes of Eden
Throne of Light
The Alchemist's Cost
Ashes of Ambition

Table of Contents

Prologue

The villa perched timelessly on the cliffs of Castelmare, where the sky met the sea in an endless embrace. The cypress trees stood tall and resolute, their whispers carried by the wind, guarding the stories carved into the villa's ancient stones. At dusk, the golden hour bathed the estate in hues of amber and rose, and the air seemed to hum with memories—of lives lived, loves lost, and truths concealed.

Elena Marconi ascended the grand staircase with measured steps, her fingertips grazing the bannister's smooth wood. It was a path she had walked often in the past year, yet tonight it felt different. The villa, with its stately silence, seemed to hold its breath as she carried an envelope—thin and unassuming, but weighty with promise.

The handwriting on the front was elegant and unmistakable: To Elena, when you are ready.

She paused at the threshold of the library, where the arched window framed the cliffs plunging into the sea below. Nico's favorite spot. For an instant, she could almost see him there—leaning casually, his hands in his pockets, his eyes fixed on the horizon. The thought steadied her.

Elena stepped into the room, where the scent of aged books and polished wood wrapped around her like a familiar embrace. She sank into the chair by the window, the envelope trembling slightly in her grasp. With a steadying breath, she broke the seal and unfolded the parchment within.

Her grandmother Livia's words unfurled across the page, delicate yet unwavering.

My dearest Elena,

If you are reading this, then the villa has given you what it once gave me—a place to discover who you are, to love without fear, and to confront the parts of yourself you've hidden away.

Elena's vision blurred as tears pricked her eyes. She wiped them hastily, her grip tightening on the letter.

I left you the villa because I knew you would hear its whispers, as I once did, and that you would have the courage to answer them. But there is one more truth I must ask you to uncover. Go to the cove—the place where my story began and ended. What you find there will not only explain my choices but, I hope, guide your own.

Elena's breath hitched, the letter trembling in her hands. The cove. She had been there before, unearthing fragments of Livia's story, letters steeped in longing and sacrifice. Yet this letter hinted at something more—a final truth waiting to be revealed.

The soft creak of the library door pulled her from her thoughts. She turned to see Nico standing in the doorway, his steady presence grounding her.

"Are you ready?" he asked, his voice low but certain.

She nodded, folding the letter back into its envelope. "I don't know what we'll find," she admitted, her voice trembling with equal parts fear and anticipation.

Nico crossed the room and took her hand, his touch warm and steady. "Whatever it is, we'll face it together."

They stepped into the courtyard, where the cypress trees swayed gently in the evening breeze, their shadows etched against the last light of day. Behind them, the villa loomed, a steadfast guardian of secrets and possibilities.

Elena tightened her grip on Nico's hand, her heart beating in rhythm with the distant crash of the waves. The whispers of the past had called her here, and she was ready to listen.

Chapter 1: Whispers on the Wind

The waves crashed against the cliffs below Castelmare, their rhythm unchanging, like a heartbeat anchoring the land to the sea. Elena Marconi leaned against the balcony's wrought-iron railing, her eyes tracing the horizon where the endless blue met the morning sky. The cypress trees whispered softly in the breeze, their murmurs carrying an unspoken call—a reminder of the letter now tucked safely in her pocket.

She unfolded it, her grandmother Livia's handwriting looping elegantly across the page. The cove—the place where my story began and ended. It had been a year since Elena first uncovered fragments of Livia and Angelo's love story, piecing together the truth behind the villa's enduring legacy. Yet this new letter suggested that the past held more—something vital still buried beneath the surface.

"Elena?"

Nico's voice broke through her thoughts. She turned to see him standing in the doorway to the balcony, a mug of espresso in his hand. His hair was slightly mussed, and the faint shadow of stubble softened the intensity of his gaze. He looked as though he hadn't quite woken up, but his presence was grounding, as always.

"Morning," she said, slipping the letter back into her pocket.

He stepped closer, handing her the mug. "You didn't come to bed last night."

She offered him a faint smile, the weight of the letter pressing against her heart. "I couldn't sleep."

"The letter?" he asked, his voice quiet but certain.

She nodded, cradling the mug between her hands. "Livia wants me to go back to the cove. She says there's something else there."

Nico frowned, his dark brows drawing together in thought. "Do you think it's safe? Last time..."

He didn't finish the sentence, but the memory was sharp in her mind. The last time they visited the cove, they had unearthed Marcello's final letter to Livia—an act that almost cost them the villa to developers eager to erase its legacy. The stakes had been high then, and they felt just as high now.

"I don't know," Elena admitted, her voice soft. "But I have to go."

Nico studied her for a moment, his expression unreadable, before he nodded. "Then we'll go."

She set the mug on the railing and reached for his hand, their fingers intertwining. The gesture was small but reassuring, a reminder of the partnership they had built over the past year. For so long, she had run from Castelmare, from the villa, and from Nico. Now, she was learning what it meant to stay.

The wind picked up, carrying the salty tang of the sea and the faint scent of wildflowers. The cypress trees swayed gently, their movements deliberate, as though urging her forward. Elena felt the weight of their whispers settle over her.

Go, they seemed to say. The past is waiting.

The small boat rocked gently as Nico steered it along the jagged coastline. The engine's low hum blended with the rhythmic crash of the waves, a steady soundtrack to their journey. Elena sat at the bow, her hands resting on the edge as the wind whipped through her hair. The letter was folded neatly in her pocket, its presence a quiet reminder of the task ahead.

The cove came into view slowly, a secluded inlet carved into the cliffs as though the earth itself had conspired to hide it. Elena felt her breath catch as they approached, the memories of her last visit rushing back. The joy of discovery. The ache of Livia's sacrifices. The sharp sting of almost losing it all.

Nico cut the engine, letting the boat drift closer to the shore. "Here we are," he said, his voice low.

Elena climbed out carefully, her boots crunching against the pebbled sand. The air here felt heavier, charged with something intangible. She walked toward the cliffs, where a jagged outcropping of rocks jutted into the sea. It was here, on this very spot, that she had found Marcello's letter. But now, the place seemed different, as though it had been waiting for her return.

A glint of light caught her eye—a small, weathered box nestled in the rocks. Her heart raced as she crouched down, lifting it carefully from its resting place. The box was heavier than it looked, its edges worn smooth by time.

"What is it?" Nico asked, his voice close behind her.

"I don't know," Elena murmured, her fingers trembling as she unlatched the box.

Inside was a folded piece of parchment, yellowed with age. Beneath it lay a locket—its tarnished silver surface familiar, a relic she had seen countless times in photographs of Livia. Her breath caught as she opened the locket, revealing a tiny photograph inside. Two figures stood together, their faces partially obscured by shadows. The woman was unmistakable—Livia.

But the man beside her wasn't Marcello.

Chapter 2: Shadows of the Past

The locket sat heavy in Elena's palm, its tarnished silver warm against her skin despite the evening's cool breeze. She stared at the photograph inside, her heart hammering as though trying to match the rhythm of the distant waves crashing against the cliffs. The image was old, slightly blurred, but unmistakably her grandmother Livia stood there. Beside her was a man Elena didn't recognize—one who wasn't Marcello.

"Elena?" Nico's voice broke through her thoughts, his presence grounding her as always. He crouched beside her, his brows drawn in concern. "What is it?"

Wordlessly, she tilted the locket so he could see. Her voice wavered as she explained. "It's Livia, but... this man—he's not Marcello."

Nico leaned closer, his expression shifting from concern to curiosity. "Are you certain? Could it be Marcello from a different time, maybe before—"

"No." She cut him off, shaking her head. "Marcello's face had a gentleness. This man... there's something sharper about him. His features are more defined—intense." Her thumb brushed over the small glass cover protecting the photograph. "I don't recognize him."

They sat in silence, the weight of this new mystery pressing down on both of them. Around them, the cypress trees swayed gently, their whispers carried by the salty breeze. It was as though the land itself wanted to offer an answer but could only hint at the truth.

Nico shifted his gaze to the weathered parchment lying in the box, its edges curling slightly with age. "Maybe the letter will explain."

Elena hesitated, her fingers hovering over the delicate paper. The last year had unraveled so much about her grandmother's life—secrets that were bittersweet, full of love, loss, and resilience. Every revelation felt like peeling back another layer of Livia's heart. But with each layer came the risk of heartbreak, and Elena wasn't sure how much more she could bear.

"Whatever it says, we'll face it together," Nico said softly, his voice steady. His hand came to rest lightly on her arm, the warmth of his touch a reminder of the partnership they'd built since she first returned to Castelmare.

Taking a deep breath, Elena nodded and unfolded the letter. The ink had faded in places, but Livia's handwriting was unmistakable—elegant and precise, each word chosen with care.

My dearest Elena,

If you have found this, it means the villa has spoken to you as it once spoke to me. It has revealed fragments of my heart that I thought would remain hidden forever.

Elena's breath hitched as she read. The letter was not simply an explanation—it was a confession.

You know of Marcello and the love we shared. But my story was not his alone. Before him, there was another—a man who shaped my life in ways I am still reckoning with.

Her grip on the parchment tightened as the world seemed to tilt beneath her. The wind picked up, carrying with it the faint scent of wildflowers and the salty tang of the sea. She glanced at Nico, whose steady gaze encouraged her to keep going.

His name was Angelo. He was not gentle, nor was he easy to love. But he was fire when my world felt cold, and he taught me how to fight for what I believed in. I have wondered for years if meeting him was fate or folly.

Elena could feel her pulse in her fingertips as she read, the words pulling her deeper into a part of Livia's life she had never imagined.

There is something you must find, hidden in the villa. It belongs to him—and to me—and it holds a truth that may help you understand not only who I was, but who you are.

The letter ended abruptly, as though Livia had written it in haste or found the words too difficult to finish. Elena stared at the page, her thoughts spinning like the wind whipping through the cypress trees.

"Angelo," she murmured, testing the name on her tongue. It felt foreign, like a story she wasn't sure she had the right to tell.

Nico broke the silence. "Do you think the villa will give you more clues?"

She folded the letter carefully, tucking it back into its envelope. "If Livia believed so, then I have to trust her. She wanted me to find this—wanted me to know about Angelo."

Nico nodded, his expression contemplative. "Do you think this changes how we see her? Or Marcello?"

"I don't know," she admitted. "It changes something. But whether it changes everything..." Her voice trailed off as she looked back toward the cliffs, where the waves continued their endless dance with the shore.

The locket, still clutched in her palm, felt heavier now—its secrets more complex than a simple photograph. She held it up to the light, studying the faint glint of silver against the fading sun.

"Livia left this for a reason," Elena said. "I need to find out why."

As they made their way back toward the villa, Elena felt the weight of her grandmother's words settle over her. She couldn't shake the feeling that the story of Angelo and Livia was more than just a chapter from the past. It was a thread, woven into the very fabric of who she was and who she might become.

The cypress trees swayed as the wind whispered around them, carrying echoes of the past. Somewhere deep within the villa's walls, Elena knew, the answers awaited.

And this time, she would listen.

Chapter 3: The Cove's Secrets

The cove stretched before Elena like a secret untold, its rocky outcroppings rising from the restless sea. The sun had dipped low in the sky, its light casting the cliffs in hues of gold and shadow. The air was cool, carrying the briny tang of salt and the faint scent of wild thyme. She stood at the water's edge, the letter from Livia folded tightly in her pocket, and let the rhythmic crash of waves steady her thoughts.

"This place..." Elena murmured, her gaze tracing the jagged shoreline. "It feels alive."

Nico stepped beside her, his boots crunching softly against the pebbled sand. "More like it's holding its breath," he said, his tone thoughtful. "Waiting."

She nodded, knowing he was right. The cove felt charged, as though the past lingered just beneath its surface, waiting to be unearthed. It was here that she had found Marcello's final letter a year ago. That discovery had been bittersweet, pulling back the veil on her grandmother's life but also leaving her with questions that seemed to multiply with each new revelation.

And now, Angelo.

Elena's hand tightened around the locket she had carried back from the cliffs. The photograph of her grandmother and the mysterious man had unsettled her, casting her memories of Livia in a new light. Who had he been? What had he meant to Livia? The letter had given no clear answers—only a tantalizing promise of more to be discovered.

"Ready?" Nico asked gently, drawing her back to the present.

She inhaled deeply and nodded. "Let's see what else she left for us."

They began their search at the base of the cliffs, where the rocks jutted out like teeth against the waves. The tide was lower now, exposing hidden crevices and narrow inlets. Elena's boots slipped on the damp stones as she moved carefully along the shoreline, her eyes scanning every crack and hollow for something out of place.

"Livia must have hidden something here," she said aloud, more to herself than to Nico. "The way she wrote about this cove—it wasn't just a setting for her story. It was important."

Nico, who had taken to prying apart clusters of driftwood with a small pocketknife, nodded in agreement. "If it's anything like last time, she probably tucked it away somewhere only she could find it."

Elena stopped beside a smooth boulder, its surface weathered by centuries of waves. The sunlight glinted off something small and metallic wedged in a crevice at its base. Her heart leapt as she crouched down, carefully working her fingers into the gap. A faint gasp escaped her lips as she pulled free a small, rusted box.

"Nico!" she called, holding it up.

He was at her side in moments, brushing sand from his hands. "What is it?"

Elena turned the box over in her hands. Its edges were worn smooth by time, and the lock on its front had long since rusted away. The lid creaked as she pried it open, revealing its contents: a delicate bracelet and a folded piece of parchment.

The bracelet gleamed faintly in the sunlight, its silver chain adorned with tiny charms—each one intricately etched with symbols she didn't immediately recognize. A tiny bird. A cypress tree. A crescent moon. The craftsmanship was exquisite, yet it felt deeply personal, as though it had been made with care and intention.

Elena set the bracelet aside and unfolded the parchment. Her breath caught as she recognized Livia's handwriting.

My dearest Elena,

If you are reading this, it means you have followed the threads I left behind. You have listened to the whispers of the villa, of the cove, and of your heart.

This bracelet was a gift from Angelo—a promise he made to me, one he could not keep. Each charm tells a piece of our story. The cypress for Castelmare. The bird for freedom. The moon for the nights we spent dreaming of a life we couldn't have.

Elena's hands trembled as she read. The bracelet, so small and delicate, seemed to hold the weight of an entire life.

Angelo taught me to be bold. To fight for what I wanted, even when it seemed impossible. But he also taught me the cost of such boldness. When you wear this bracelet, remember that strength does not come without sacrifice. And that sometimes, letting go is the most courageous act of all.

There is one more thing you must find. In the villa, hidden in the study, there is a journal—Angelo's. It contains the truths I could not bear to write here. Find it, Elena. Only then will you understand.

The letter ended abruptly, as if Livia had struggled with the decision to write it at all. Elena lowered the parchment, her heart heavy with questions. Angelo's journal? What truths could it hold that Livia hadn't already revealed?

Nico touched her shoulder lightly. "Are you okay?"

She nodded, though her thoughts were a storm. "I need to go back to the villa. If what she said is true, the answers are there."

"What do you think Angelo meant to her?" Nico asked, his voice soft. "Do you think he was... more important than Marcello?"

Elena traced her thumb over the bracelet's charms, their edges smooth beneath her touch. "I don't know. But if he wasn't, he was something just as significant. He shaped her, Nico—who she was, the choices she made. And now he's shaping me."

The walk back to the boat was quiet, each step heavy with the weight of discovery. The sun had nearly set, casting the cove in deep purples and blues. As they boarded the small vessel, Elena turned for one last look at the rocky inlet. The cove seemed to shimmer in the twilight, as though it, too, carried the memory of what had transpired there.

As Nico steered them back toward Castelmare, Elena clutched the bracelet in her hand, the charms clinking softly. She couldn't help but feel that the past was no longer a distant echo but a part of her present, intertwining her story with Livia's in ways she was only beginning to understand.

The cypress trees loomed on the cliffs above, their shadows stretching long over the villa. Elena's heart swelled with equal parts fear and determination. Whatever truths Angelo's journal held, she was ready to uncover them.

Chapter 4: Angelo's Truth

The villa was quiet as Elena and Nico made their way to the east wing. Their footsteps echoed softly against the marble floor, the air heavy with anticipation. Elena held the silver key tightly in her hand, its smooth surface warming against her skin. Each step brought her closer to a truth she wasn't sure she was ready to uncover.

The door stood at the end of the corridor, unassuming and aged. Its brass handle gleamed faintly in the dim light. Elena hesitated as she reached it, her chest tightening with a mix of fear and determination.

"Ready?" Nico asked, his voice low but steady.

She nodded, slipping the key into the lock. It turned smoothly, the mechanism clicking with a sound that seemed impossibly loud in the silence. She pushed the door open, and a rush of cool air greeted them, carrying the faint scent of cedar and salt.

The room beyond was small but meticulously preserved. A desk sat in the center, its surface covered with neatly arranged papers, an oil lamp, and a journal with a leather cover. Shelves lined the walls, filled with books and artifacts that seemed out of place in the villa—a collection of maps, resistance insignias, and faded photographs.

Elena's breath caught as she stepped inside, her gaze falling on a large photograph framed above the desk. It was a group portrait of men and women standing together, their expressions a mix of defiance and determination. Angelo stood at the center, his intense eyes staring directly at the camera.

"This was his," Elena whispered, her fingers brushing the edge of the desk. "This room—it was his."

Nico moved to the shelves, inspecting the maps and documents. "Looks like he was keeping records. Of what, though?"

Elena picked up the journal, her fingers trembling as she opened it. The handwriting inside was angular and hurried—Angelo's words spilling across the pages as though he had written them in haste.

April 1943

The resistance grows stronger, but so do the dangers. Whispers of betrayal reach my ears daily, and I fear the cracks in our foundation are widening. I trust few, but Livia remains my constant. Her love is my anchor, even as the world crumbles around us.

Elena paused, her chest tightening as she read his words. "He was part of the resistance," she murmured, her voice barely above a whisper. "But he knew there were dangers—betrayals."

Nico frowned, pulling a document from one of the shelves. "It looks like he kept track of troop movements. Maybe he was feeding this information to the resistance?"

Elena nodded, flipping to another entry.

May 1943

They came to the villa last night—soldiers searching for names, for proof. Livia gave them what they wanted, but at a cost. I saw the pain in her eyes as she lied, as she betrayed someone else to protect me. I wanted to stop her, but she was relentless. She saved me, but I fear I've broken her heart in return.

Elena's breath hitched as the words settled over her. "She lied to protect him," she said, her voice trembling. "She gave up someone else's name to keep him safe."

Nico's jaw tightened. "Who? Did he say?"

Elena shook her head, turning the pages quickly, searching for more answers. The next entry was shorter, but the weight of its words struck her like a blow.

June 1943

The betrayal came from within. A name whispered in shadows, traded for safety or power. Massimo, my closest friend, my brother in arms, sold us out. I can't stay—not with Livia tied to me. If they find me, they'll destroy her too. Leaving is the only way to keep her safe, even if it means breaking both our hearts.

Elena lowered the journal, her vision blurring with tears. The pieces were falling into place, but the picture they formed was devastating. Angelo hadn't just left because of the danger. He had left because he loved Livia too much to let her be caught in the crossfire of his life.

"She knew," Elena said softly. "She must have known he left to protect her."

Nico stepped closer, his hand resting lightly on her shoulder. "And she kept his secret all these years. Maybe because she knew it was the only way to honor him."

Elena nodded, her fingers brushing the journal's pages. "But it wasn't just love. It was guilt. He couldn't forgive himself for what she sacrificed for him."

Later That Evening

Elena sat in the library, the journal and letters spread before her. The locket lay beside them, its tarnished silver catching the flicker of candlelight. She traced the edges of the journal, her thoughts tangled with the weight of Angelo's choices and Livia's sacrifices.

Nico entered the room, carrying two glasses of wine. He set one in front of her, his expression calm but searching. "You've been quiet," he said gently.

"There's so much," Elena murmured, her voice heavy with emotion. "So much they gave up. For love, for safety, for survival. I don't know how they carried it all."

Nico sat beside her, his hand covering hers. "They carried it because they had each other, even when they were apart."

Elena met his gaze, her chest tightening with gratitude for his steady presence. "Do you think he ever forgave himself?"

Nico's brow furrowed in thought. "Maybe. Or maybe he didn't need to. Sometimes love isn't about forgiveness—it's about understanding."

Elena looked down at the journal, her fingers brushing the worn leather. "I understand now. I understand her. And him."

The villa's walls seemed to hum around her, their silence heavy but not oppressive. For the first time, Elena felt like she was beginning to grasp the legacy Livia had left her—not just a story of love and loss, but of resilience and the courage to endure.

As the night deepened, Elena closed the journal, her resolve hardening. There was more to uncover, more to piece together. But for now, she let the villa's quiet embrace lull her, the whispers of its past no longer haunting, but comforting.

Chapter 5: The Villa's Walls

The villa loomed quietly in the pale morning light, its ivy-draped walls bathed in hues of gold. Elena stood in the courtyard, her hand resting against the weathered stone. The texture was cool beneath her fingers, grounding her in the present, but the weight of the journal in her other hand anchored her in the past. Each word within it unraveled what she thought she knew about her grandmother, Livia, and the man she had loved, Angelo.

"Elena," Nico called from the veranda, his voice soft but steady. He carried two mugs of coffee, their steam curling in the crisp air like delicate whispers.

She turned, managing a faint smile as he approached. "I couldn't sleep," she admitted, taking one of the mugs. The warmth seeped into her hands, a small comfort against the chill that had taken root in her chest.

"Thinking about the journal?" he asked, though his tone suggested he already knew the answer.

Elena nodded, her gaze drifting toward the cliffs where the sea stretched endlessly. "Angelo carried so much. And Livia—she gave up so much for him. It's all there in his words, but I feel like I'm only scratching the surface."

Nico leaned against the stone wall beside her, his eyes searching hers. "The truth is heavy," he said. "But you don't have to carry it alone."

His words settled over her like the first rays of sunlight, warming her from the inside out. She nodded, grateful for his quiet strength, and sipped her coffee, letting the villa's stillness envelop them. Yet the stillness didn't feel empty—it felt alive, as though the villa itself was watching, waiting.

Later That Morning

The library was bathed in sunlight when Elena returned, golden beams illuminating dust motes that danced lazily in the air. The journal and letters lay open on the desk, flanked by photographs of Angelo and Livia. The room felt alive with their presence, as though the villa's walls were steeped in their memories.

Elena's fingers traced the edges of a map Angelo had sketched, his notes scrawled in the margins. The lines told a story of strategy and survival, but they also hinted at the burden of a man who had fought for a freedom he might never live to see.

"What are you looking for?" Nico asked, stepping into the room.

She glanced up, her brow furrowed. "I don't know. Something to make sense of it all. Livia kept so much hidden, but now that I know about Angelo's room, I feel like the villa might hold more than just their story. Maybe it's kept pieces of everyone who's ever lived here."

Nico tilted his head thoughtfully. "The villa's seen generations of love and loss. Maybe that's why it feels alive—like it's holding on to everything."

Elena tilted her head, considering his words. "Do you think that's why she left it to me? Because she wanted me to find these pieces?"

"Maybe," Nico said, his voice quiet but steady. "Or maybe she wanted you to add your own story to it."

The thought sent a shiver through her—not of fear, but of recognition. The villa wasn't just a monument to the past. It was a living legacy, and now she was a part of it.

That Afternoon

Elena found herself in the courtyard again, this time with Nico at her side. The cypress trees swayed gently in the breeze, their shadows stretching long and thin across the cobblestones. The air smelled of salt and jasmine, a heady mix that always reminded her of summers spent chasing sunlight through the villa's gardens.

"What now?" Nico asked, his voice low.

Elena turned to him, her eyes steady. "We search. If Angelo's journal and Livia's letters have taught me anything, it's that the villa is as much a part of their story as they were of its. There's more here. I can feel it."

They began in the great hall, their footsteps echoing softly as they moved from one end to the other. Nico inspected the fireplace, running his hands along its ornate carvings, while Elena traced the edges of the wainscoting, searching for any sign of hidden compartments or loose panels.

"What if it's not in the library or the hall?" Nico asked after a while. "What if it's somewhere less obvious?"

Elena straightened, her thoughts racing. "The chapel."

He looked at her, his brow furrowing. "The chapel?"

She nodded. "It's barely been touched in years. But Livia always went there when she needed clarity. If she left something behind, it would be there."

The Chapel

The chapel was tucked away near the villa's southern edge, its stone walls overgrown with ivy. Inside, the air was cool and still, carrying the faint scent of candle wax and wood. Sunlight streamed through the stained-glass windows, casting fractured rainbows across the floor.

Elena knelt near the altar, her fingers brushing the base of the wooden structure. "Help me move this," she said, glancing at Nico.

Together, they shifted the altar slightly, revealing a small trapdoor hidden beneath. Elena's heart raced as she lifted it, revealing a shallow compartment filled with carefully wrapped bundles.

"What is it?" Nico asked, crouching beside her.

Elena unwrapped one of the bundles, her breath catching as she uncovered a collection of letters tied with a faded ribbon. Each one bore Angelo's name in Livia's elegant handwriting.

"She kept them," Elena murmured, her voice trembling. "All of his letters. She never let them go."

Nico placed a hand on her back, his touch steadying. "She loved him, even when he wasn't here."

Elena nodded, tears pricking her eyes as she cradled the letters. The chapel's stillness seemed to echo with the weight of Livia's love, her sacrifices, and her resilience. And as Elena held the letters close, she felt the villa's walls hum with quiet approval, as though it, too, recognized the magnitude of the discovery.

That Evening

As the sun dipped below the horizon, casting the villa in soft twilight, Elena sat in the courtyard with Nico. The letters lay between them, their faded ink a testament to a love that had endured despite the odds.

"What will you do with them?" Nico asked, his voice gentle.

Elena looked at the bundle, her fingers brushing the ribbon. "I'll keep them. Not just for Livia or Angelo, but for everyone who's lived here. Their stories deserve to be remembered."

Nico smiled faintly, his gaze soft. "And what about your story? Where does it go from here?"

Elena met his eyes, her chest tightening with a mix of fear and hope. "I don't know," she admitted. "But I think it starts here. With this villa, with everything it's taught me."

As the first stars appeared in the sky, Elena felt a sense of peace settle over her. The villa's walls had carried generations of love and loss, but now, they carried her story too. And beneath the cypress sky, she was ready to embrace whatever came next.

Chapter 6: Echoes in the Attic

The attic was dimly lit, the single bulb overhead casting long shadows that danced across the wooden beams. The scent of aged wood and mothballs clung to the air, mingling with the faint salt tang that seemed to permeate the entire villa. Elena stood at the threshold, her heart pounding as her eyes adjusted to the gloom. The space stretched out before her, cluttered with trunks, boxes, and forgotten heirlooms shrouded in layers of dust.

Behind her, Nico's steady footsteps creaked on the narrow staircase. "This place feels like a time capsule," he said, his voice low, as though not to disturb the ghosts of the past.

Elena nodded, stepping cautiously into the room. "It is. Livia used to say the attic was where the past lived. I didn't understand what she meant... until now."

She swept her gaze over the room, her chest tightening at the weight of untold stories buried in this forgotten space. Together, they began their search, their movements careful as they sifted through the accumulated remnants of generations. Dust motes swirled in the dim light, disturbed by their quiet progress.

Elena opened a small chest filled with faded linens, her fingers brushing against delicate lace and embroidery that had yellowed with time. Beneath the fabric, she caught a glint of something dark. She paused, her breath catching as she pulled free a photograph tucked between the folds.

The image was black-and-white, its edges frayed, the faces within illuminated by stark sunlight. A group of people stood near the cliffs, their expressions a mixture of defiance and hope. At the center was Angelo, his arm resting lightly on Livia's shoulder. Her smile was faint, almost hesitant, but filled with a kind of love that made Elena's chest ache.

"Look at this," she murmured, holding the photograph out for Nico to see.

He crouched beside her, leaning closer. "That's them," he said, his brow furrowing as he studied their faces. "Angelo and Livia."

Elena nodded, her gaze lingering on her grandmother's expression. "She looks so happy, but... there's something else. It's like she knew it couldn't last."

"Maybe she did," Nico said thoughtfully. "Maybe they both did."

An Hour Later

The attic seemed endless, a labyrinth of trunks and boxes revealing fragments of the lives that had passed through the villa. But it wasn't until Elena reached the far corner that she found what she didn't know she'd been looking for.

A wooden chest, smaller than the others, sat half-hidden beneath a faded quilt. Its surface was carved with intricate designs—cypress trees and swirling waves, their patterns worn smooth by time. Elena knelt before it, her fingers trembling as she brushed the dust away.

"This is it," she whispered.

Nico crouched beside her, his expression curious. "How do you know?"

"Because it's hers," Elena said, her voice firm despite the tremor in her hands. "I remember this chest. It was in her room when I was a child. I didn't know she moved it here."

She unlatched the chest carefully, the hinges groaning as she lifted the lid. Inside, the contents were wrapped in cloth and paper, their edges frayed with age. Elena's breath caught as she uncovered a leather-bound notebook, its cover embossed with Livia's initials.

"It's her journal," she murmured, her hands trembling as she opened it.

Livia's Journal

The pages were filled with Livia's elegant handwriting, the ink looping in deliberate strokes. Elena scanned the entries, her pulse quickening as fragments of a story she had only begun to understand unfolded before her.

April 1943

I met Angelo beneath the cypress trees today. He was agitated, pacing as he spoke of the resistance and the dangers they faced. His passion is a fire, one that burns brightly but consumes everything around it. I fear for him, but I fear for myself more—for the way my heart races in his presence, for the way I cannot imagine a life without him.

May 1943

The soldiers came to the villa last night. Angelo had warned me they might, but I wasn't prepared for their questions, their threats. They were looking for him, for proof of his involvement. I gave them nothing, but the look in their eyes told me they didn't believe me. Angelo said he would leave if it became too dangerous, but how can I let him go?

Elena's fingers tightened on the edges of the journal as her chest ached with each word. "She loved him so much," she murmured, her voice breaking slightly.

Nico placed a hand on her shoulder, his touch grounding. "But it wasn't enough to keep him here."

Elena nodded, flipping carefully to the next page.

June 1943

The night he left, I stood beneath the cypress trees and watched him disappear into the darkness. He said it was for my safety, but it felt like a betrayal. I wanted to call him back, to tell him that nothing was worth this pain. But I stayed silent, and now I live with the echoes of his absence.

Elena closed the journal, her fingers clutching the worn leather cover as tears blurred her vision. "She never stopped loving him," she whispered.

"And he never stopped loving her," Nico said softly, crouching beside her. "That much is clear."

Elena looked at him, her chest tight with emotion. "But they couldn't stay together. Everything was against them."

Nico's gaze was steady. "Sometimes love isn't enough to overcome the world. But that doesn't make it any less real."

That Evening

The attic felt different as Elena and Nico descended the narrow staircase, the journal and photograph cradled in her arms. The weight of the past lingered, but it no longer felt oppressive. Instead, it felt like a gift—a story waiting to be honored.

In the library, Elena spread the items across the desk. The journal sat in the center, its pages filled with Livia's voice. The photograph lay beside it, a snapshot of a love that had defied the odds, even if it hadn't endured.

"What will you do with it?" Nico asked, his tone gentle.

Elena traced the edges of the photograph, her expression thoughtful. "I think I need to share it. Livia's story, Angelo's story—it's part of the villa's history. But it's also part of Castelmare's history. It belongs to all of us."

Nico smiled faintly, his hand brushing hers. "They'd be proud of you."

Elena looked at him, her chest swelling with gratitude. "Thank you. For being here. For helping me carry this."

"You're not alone in this, Elena," he said, his smile deepening. "You never have been."

As the last rays of sunlight faded from the sky, Elena felt a quiet resolve settle over her. The attic had given up its secrets, and the villa's walls seemed to hum with approval. There was more to uncover, but for the first time, she felt ready.

Chapter 7: Beneath the Cypress Sky

The cypress trees swayed gently in the evening breeze, their tall, slender silhouettes etched against the violet sky. Elena stood beneath them, her grandmother's journal cradled in her arms. The salt-tinged air wrapped around her, carrying whispers she couldn't quite decipher but felt deeply.

She traced the cover of the journal with her fingers, its worn leather smooth and familiar. Since uncovering it in the attic, she had spent hours poring over its pages, immersing herself in Livia's words. The love her grandmother had shared with Angelo was raw and consuming, a flame that burned brightly even as it devoured them.

"Elena." Nico's voice came softly from behind her.

She turned to see him approaching, his steps measured. He carried a small lantern, its warm glow casting golden light across his face. "You've been out here a while," he said gently.

"I needed to be," she replied, her voice steady but low. "This place—it's where they always met. It's where she said goodbye to him."

Nico nodded, his gaze shifting to the trees. "And now it's part of your story, too."

She let out a soft breath, her chest tightening with the weight of his words. "It doesn't feel like mine yet. It feels like theirs—like I'm just a guest in their legacy."

He stepped closer, the lantern's glow illuminating the space between them. "Maybe that's how it starts. You honor their story, and in doing so, you find your own."

Elena looked down at the journal, her fingers brushing its edges. "I want to know everything," she murmured. "Not just about them, but about this place. The villa, the trees, the lives that have passed through here. It's all connected."

Nico tilted his head, a faint smile tugging at his lips. "Then let's start now."

An Unlikely Revelation

Together, they began exploring the grove of cypress trees. The ground was uneven, the earth cool beneath their feet as they searched for something—anything—that might offer new insights. Elena's mind raced with fragments of Livia's journal, her words looping endlessly.

We buried it beneath the cypress sky. It was the only way to keep it safe.

She paused near the largest tree, its gnarled roots twisting like ancient veins. "This one," she said, her voice filled with certainty. "She always wrote about this tree. It's where they made their promises."

Nico crouched beside the roots, holding the lantern aloft. "If they hid something here, it would've been well concealed."

Elena knelt beside him, her fingers brushing the damp earth. The journal's cryptic mention of something buried had been haunting her since she first read it. Could it be here? Could the answers she sought be lying just beneath the surface?

Nico reached for a small spade he'd brought, the blade glinting faintly in the lantern light. Together, they began digging, the soft earth yielding easily beneath their hands.

Minutes passed, the silence broken only by the rhythmic scrape of the spade and their steady breathing.

And then, the blade hit something solid.

Elena froze, her heart racing. "Did you feel that?"

Nico nodded, his movements careful as he cleared the surrounding soil. Slowly, a small wooden box emerged, its surface darkened and worn with age.

Elena's hands trembled as she lifted it free, the weight of it surprising. The box was simple, unadorned, but it felt significant in her grasp. She unlatched the clasp, her breath catching as she opened the lid.

Inside was a bundle of letters tied with a crimson ribbon, their edges yellowed with time. Beneath them lay a delicate silver ring and a small vial filled with what appeared to be dried lavender. The scent was faint but unmistakable—a fragrance that had always reminded her of Livia.

"They kept this here," Elena whispered, her voice trembling. "It must have been their way of holding on to each other."

Nico crouched beside her, his gaze steady. "Even when they were apart, they had this."

Elena lifted one of the letters, the paper soft and fragile in her hands. The words were written in Angelo's familiar scrawl.

My dearest Livia,

The world is cruel and unyielding, but you have always been my safe place. I carry you with me in everything I do, and even if I cannot return, know that my heart remains yours. Beneath this cypress sky, I leave you this promise: you will always be my beginning and my end.

Yours always, Angelo

Tears blurred Elena's vision as she read, the weight of Angelo's words settling over her like a heavy but comforting blanket. She folded the letter carefully, placing it back in the box.

"He never stopped loving her," she said, her voice thick with emotion.

"And she never stopped loving him," Nico added softly. "Even when the world kept them apart."

Elena's gaze lifted to the sky, where the cypress trees swayed gently against the rising wind. For the first time, she felt a deep connection to the love her grandmother had carried—a love that had endured despite the odds, despite the pain.

Later That Night

Back in the villa, Elena placed the box on the desk in the library. The letters, the ring, the vial of lavender—they were pieces of a story that had shaped her family, fragments of a love that had persisted against all reason.

Nico stood by the window, his silhouette outlined by the pale moonlight. "What will you do with it?" he asked, his voice calm.

Elena turned to him, her chest tightening with resolve. "I'll keep it. But I'll also share it. Livia and Angelo's story deserves to be remembered, not just by me, but by everyone who loves this villa."

Nico smiled faintly, his gaze softening. "And your story? Where does it go from here?"

Elena met his eyes, her heart swelling with a mix of fear and hope. "I think it starts here. With this villa, with everything it's taught me about love, resilience, and sacrifice."

The villa seemed to hum softly around her, its walls carrying the echoes of generations. And as she stood beneath the cypress sky, Elena felt ready—ready to carry the legacy forward, to let it shape her own story, and to embrace whatever came next.

Chapter 8: A Legacy to Keep

The villa was bathed in the soft, golden light of late afternoon, the shadows of the cypress trees stretching long across the courtyard. Elena sat at the library desk, the wooden box from the grove resting before her. The letters, the silver ring, and the vial of lavender were now carefully arranged, their presence filling the room with a quiet weight.

She traced the edges of the ring with her fingertips, its cool surface smooth and worn. This simple object, so small and delicate, held a story of love and promises that had spanned decades. It felt impossibly fragile, yet unyielding—much like the love it represented.

"You've been quiet," Nico said, stepping into the room. He carried two glasses of wine, setting one beside her before taking a seat across from her. His presence, as steady as the villa itself, filled the space with a calm she had come to rely on.

"I've been thinking," Elena replied, her voice soft but steady. "About everything—Livia, Angelo, the villa. It feels like I've been handed this enormous responsibility, and I'm not sure I know what to do with it."

Nico leaned forward, his dark eyes searching hers. "You've already done more than you realize. You've uncovered their story, pieced together the fragments they left behind. That's no small thing."

Elena managed a faint smile, lifting her glass to her lips. The wine's rich, earthy flavor grounded her, anchoring her in the present even as her thoughts swirled with the weight of the past.

"I just don't want to let them down," she admitted, her voice barely above a whisper.

"You won't," Nico said firmly. "You've honored them with every step you've taken."

A Decision Made

As the sun dipped lower in the sky, Elena and Nico walked through the villa, their footsteps echoing softly in the quiet halls. The journal, letters, and artifacts from the grove weighed on Elena's mind, but alongside the weight was a growing sense of clarity.

They paused in the main hall, where a grand portrait of Livia hung above the mantel. Her eyes seemed to meet Elena's, their expression calm yet knowing, as though she had always understood that this moment would come.

"This villa was her sanctuary," Elena said, her voice thoughtful. "But it was also her prison. She stayed here, carried the weight of her choices, and kept Angelo's story alive. I can't let it end with me."

Nico tilted his head, his gaze steady. "What are you thinking?"

Elena turned to him, her chest tightening with resolve. "I'm going to write her story. Their story. It's the only way to keep it alive, to make sure it's not forgotten."

A smile tugged at Nico's lips, warm and genuine. "I think she'd be proud of that."

"I hope so," Elena said softly. "It's the least I can do for her—for both of them."

The First Words

That evening, Elena sat in the library with her laptop open before her. The letters, journal, and photograph were arranged neatly on the desk, their presence a quiet encouragement. The cypress trees outside swayed gently in the moonlight, their silhouettes framed by the arched windows.

She placed her hands on the keyboard, her fingers hovering for a moment as she considered how to begin. The story felt vast and intricate, its threads stretching across generations. But as she closed her eyes, Livia's voice seemed to echo in her mind, soft but insistent.

Begin where it matters most.

Elena's fingers moved, the words flowing as if guided by the whispers of the villa itself.

Beneath the cypress sky, where the sea meets the cliffs of Castelmare, a love was forged in shadows and sacrifice. This is the story of Livia and Angelo, and the legacy they left behind.

The sentences felt right, their rhythm steady and true. Elena paused, her chest tightening with emotion as she reread the opening lines. This wasn't just Livia's story or Angelo's story—it was hers, too. A story of resilience, of love that endured despite impossible odds, and of a legacy that refused to fade.

Nico entered the room, his steps quiet. He stood behind her, resting his hands gently on her shoulders as he read over her work. "It's beautiful," he said softly.

Elena tilted her head back to look at him, a smile breaking through her seriousness. "It's a start."

"It's more than that," he said. "It's exactly what this place needs."

She nodded, her gaze returning to the screen. The villa, with its whispers and secrets, seemed to hum softly around her, its approval almost tangible. For the first time in years, Elena felt at peace—not just with the past, but with her place in its unfolding story.

Chapter 9: Threads Woven Together

The morning light poured through the villa's arched windows, filling the library with a warm, golden glow. Elena sat at the desk, surrounded by fragments of the past: Livia's journal, Angelo's letters, and the weathered photograph from the grove. Her laptop hummed softly, the screen glowing with the beginnings of a story she felt compelled to tell.

She ran her fingers over the silver ring that rested beside her keyboard, its cool surface grounding her. It was a small thing, almost insignificant to anyone else, but to her, it was a symbol of something much greater—love, sacrifice, and resilience.

"You've been busy," Nico said from the doorway, his voice breaking the quiet. He carried a plate of fresh fruit and pastries, setting it down on the desk beside her.

Elena smiled, grateful for his steadiness. "I didn't realize how much I had to say until I started. It's like once the words came, they wouldn't stop."

He leaned against the desk, his gaze soft but intent. "That's a good sign. It means you're telling the story the way it needs to be told."

She nodded, reaching for a piece of fruit. "It's strange. I thought writing about them would make me feel further away from their story, but it's the opposite. I feel closer to them—to Livia, to Angelo—than I ever have."

Nico's hand brushed hers briefly, a reassuring gesture. "Because you're not just writing their story. You're becoming part of it."

A Walk Through Memory

Later that morning, Elena and Nico walked through the villa's gardens, the cypress trees swaying gently above them. The scent of jasmine and lavender filled the air, mingling with the salt of the distant sea. Elena carried Livia's journal with her, its pages dog-eared from constant reading.

"I used to think the villa was just a place," she said, her voice thoughtful. "A building with walls and windows. But it's more than that. It's alive. It holds everything—every memory, every story. It's part of who I am."

Nico glanced at her, his expression warm. "And now you're part of it."

They paused beneath the largest cypress tree, its twisted roots stretching out like veins in the earth. Elena ran her hand along its bark, the rough surface grounding her.

"This is where it all began," she murmured. "For them. For me. Everything circles back to this place."

Nico nodded, his hand resting lightly on her shoulder. "Then maybe it's where everything begins again."

An Unexpected Visitor

As they returned to the villa, the sound of a car approaching the courtyard caught their attention. Elena frowned, exchanging a curious glance with Nico before stepping toward the entrance. A sleek black sedan pulled to a stop, and an older man with salt-and-pepper hair stepped out, his posture poised and elegant.

"Elena Marconi?" he asked, his voice smooth and accented.

"Yes," she replied cautiously. "And you are?"

"Pietro Romano," he said, inclining his head. "Angelo Romano was my grandfather."

Elena's breath caught, her heart racing. She felt Nico's steady presence beside her, grounding her as the revelation settled over her.

"I've been trying to find this place for years," Pietro continued, his gaze sweeping over the villa. "My grandfather spoke of it often, but he was always so careful with his words. It wasn't until recently that I found a letter he'd written to my father, detailing the villa and the woman he loved."

Elena's throat tightened as she gestured for him to follow. "Come in. There's something you need to see."

Bridging the Past and Present

In the library, Pietro sat quietly as Elena laid out the journal, letters, and photograph. His hands trembled slightly as he picked up Angelo's letters, his eyes scanning the familiar handwriting.

"This is his," Pietro said softly, his voice thick with emotion. "I never thought I'd see this—any of this."

Elena watched him closely, her own emotions tangled with the weight of the moment. "Your grandfather loved her—Livia—with everything he had. He left to protect her, but he never stopped carrying her with him."

Pietro nodded, his gaze distant. "He spoke of her often, even in his final years. He said she was the bravest woman he'd ever known."

A quiet silence fell over the room, the weight of generations settling between them. Finally, Pietro looked up, his expression resolute.

"This story—it needs to be told," he said. "Not just for them, but for everyone who carries their legacy."

Elena met his gaze, a small smile breaking through her seriousness. "That's what I'm trying to do."

A Shared Understanding

As the day wore on, Elena and Pietro walked through the villa, sharing stories and piecing together fragments of their family's intertwined histories. Nico followed quietly, his presence steady and unobtrusive, offering his thoughts when needed.

By the time Pietro left, the villa felt different to Elena—not just a place of discovery, but a bridge between past and present, between Livia and Angelo's love and the life she was building for herself.

Standing in the courtyard, Elena watched the black sedan disappear down the road. The cypress trees swayed above her, their whispers blending with the evening breeze.

"This is just the beginning," Nico said, his voice soft but sure.

Elena turned to him, her heart swelling with gratitude and hope. "It feels like it."

As they stood beneath the cypress sky, Elena felt a quiet peace settle over her. The threads of the past had woven themselves into her present, creating a tapestry of love, resilience, and connection. And as the villa's walls hummed softly around her, she knew she was exactly where she was meant to be.

Chapter 10: A New Beginning

The villa stood bathed in the warm light of late afternoon, its walls glowing with an almost golden hue. The cypress trees swayed gently in the breeze, their whispers a constant, soothing presence. Elena sat on the balcony overlooking the cliffs, the sea stretching endlessly before her. In her lap rested Livia's journal, the edges worn from weeks of careful reading.

The story she had pieced together felt complete now, though its weight lingered. Livia and Angelo's love, their sacrifices, and the legacy they had left behind were no longer just fragments of the past—they were threads woven into her present.

Nico stepped onto the balcony, carrying two cups of espresso. "You've been quiet all morning," he said, handing her one of the cups.

"I've been thinking," she replied, her voice thoughtful. "About what comes next."

He leaned against the railing, his gaze steady. "And?"

She took a sip of the espresso, the rich, bitter flavor grounding her. "I think I finally know what I want to do. I want to stay here. Not just for the villa or for Livia and Angelo's story, but for me. This place—it feels like home."

Nico smiled, his eyes warm. "I was hoping you'd say that."

Elena raised an eyebrow. "Oh?"

He shrugged, his grin widening. "I've been putting off a few projects, waiting to see if you'd decide to stay. Now I can finally get to work."

A laugh bubbled from her chest, light and unexpected. For the first time in what felt like years, the future felt full of possibility.

The Story Begins

Later that evening, Elena sat in the library, the glow of her laptop illuminating her face. The letters and journal were spread before her, their presence a steady reminder of why she had begun this journey.

Her fingers hovered over the keyboard for a moment before she began typing.

The villa on the cliffs of Castelmare had stood for generations, its walls steeped in stories of love and loss. Beneath the cypress sky, where the sea met the land, a promise was made—and that promise echoed through time.

The words flowed easily now, each keystroke pulling her deeper into the story she was determined to tell. She wrote of Livia and Angelo, of their passion and resilience, and of the villa that had held their secrets for so long. But she also wrote of herself—of her discovery, her connection to the past, and the way it had shaped her present.

Hours passed, the library bathed in the soft light of a single lamp. Nico appeared briefly, bringing her tea and a quiet smile before retreating to give her space. The villa's quiet hum seemed to envelop her, its approval almost tangible.

When she finally stopped, the first chapter was complete. She leaned back in her chair, her heart full. For the first time, she felt like she was writing not just for Livia and Angelo, but for herself—for the life she was building here in Castelmare.

A Celebration of Love

The following weekend, the villa hosted a gathering—a small celebration in honor of its legacy. Pietro Romano returned, bringing with him more stories and photographs from Angelo's life. Neighbors and friends from the village filled the courtyard, their laughter and conversation mingling with the music that drifted through the air.

Elena moved through the crowd, greeting guests and sharing snippets of the villa's history. Pietro stood near the fountain, recounting one of Angelo's tales to an enraptured audience, while Nico helped serve wine and hors d'oeuvres with an ease that made her heart swell.

As the evening wore on, Elena found herself beneath the largest cypress tree, the night sky glittering above her. Nico joined her, his presence as steady as ever.

"This feels right," she said softly, her gaze sweeping over the courtyard. "Like the villa is alive again."

"It is," Nico replied. "Because of you."

She turned to him, her chest tightening with emotion. "Because of us. I couldn't have done any of this without you."

He smiled, stepping closer. "Well, I'm not going anywhere. So what's next?"

Elena tilted her head, considering the question. "The book, of course. But after that... who knows? I think for the first time, I'm okay with not having all the answers."

Nico's smile deepened as he reached for her hand, their fingers intertwining. "Then here's to what comes next."

They stood together beneath the cypress sky, the villa's walls humming softly around them. The past had been uncovered, its stories honored. And now, the future stretched before them, open and full of promise.

Chapter 11: The Villa Speaks

The sun broke through the clouds, casting golden beams across Castelmare. The villa stood quietly beneath the sky, as though waiting for what came next. Elena paced the library, Livia's journal in one hand and a letter from Angelo in the other. Her thoughts churned with fragments of their story, each discovery a piece of a puzzle that seemed never-ending.

The door creaked softly as Nico stepped in, holding a small tray with coffee and a plate of biscotti. "You've been at this all morning," he said, setting the tray down on the desk. "Found anything new?"

Elena sighed, running her fingers through her hair. "I keep coming back to this line in the journal. She writes about the villa as if it's alive, as if it holds more than just memories."

Nico leaned against the desk, his eyes narrowing in thought. "Maybe it does. You've already uncovered more than you ever expected. Why stop now?"

She nodded, setting the journal down and picking up the photograph they'd found in the attic. Angelo and Livia stood together, their expressions full of quiet defiance. "I feel like they're telling me to keep looking. Like the villa still has secrets it hasn't revealed."

"Well, if it does, I'm sure we'll find them," Nico said with a small smile. "You're not one to give up."

Elena smiled faintly, his words a steadying force. "Let's keep searching."

A Hidden Passage

They moved through the villa systematically, room by room, searching for anything that might provide new clues. The great hall revealed nothing but dust and shadow, and the east wing, with its locked door now open, seemed to have offered all it could. Finally, they made their way to the northern wing, the oldest part of the villa.

"This wing was rarely used," Elena said as they climbed the creaking stairs. "Even when I was a child, we avoided it. It always felt... different."

Nico followed closely, the beam of his flashlight cutting through the dim hallway. "Different how?"

Elena hesitated, her hand brushing against the peeling wallpaper. "Like it didn't belong to the rest of the house. The air felt heavier, like it was keeping something in."

The northern wing was colder, the chill seeping into their bones despite the warmth of the day. The walls were lined with faded portraits, their subjects staring solemnly as though guarding long-forgotten secrets. At the end of the hallway, a door stood ajar, its hinges rusted with age.

Inside, the room was bare except for a massive armoire standing against one wall. Its surface was carved with intricate designs—cypress trees and swirling waves, like the chest they had found in the attic.

"This is it," Elena whispered, her breath catching.

Nico stepped forward, testing the armoire's doors. They opened with a groan, revealing shelves filled with books and papers. But it wasn't until he pushed aside a stack of old ledgers that he noticed something unusual.

"There's a panel here," he said, running his hand along the back of the armoire. "It looks loose."

Elena leaned in, her pulse quickening. Together, they pried the panel loose, revealing a narrow passageway behind it. The air inside was stale and damp, carrying the faint scent of earth and decay.

Nico turned to her, his flashlight cutting into the darkness. "Do we go in?"

Elena hesitated, her chest tightening with equal parts fear and curiosity. "We have to."

The Passage Beneath

The passage was narrow and steep, the stone walls cool and rough beneath their fingers as they descended. The flashlight beam illuminated the way, revealing a path that seemed to twist endlessly into the earth.

"How far does this go?" Nico asked, his voice echoing faintly.

"I don't know," Elena replied. "I didn't even know this existed."

Finally, the passage opened into a small underground chamber. The walls were lined with shelves, each one crammed with artifacts—letters, photographs, and faded documents. At the center of the room stood a wooden table, its surface covered with maps and notebooks.

Elena approached the table, her breath catching as she recognized the handwriting on one of the maps. "This is Angelo's," she whispered.

Nico moved to her side, his eyes scanning the items on the table. "These must have been his records. From the resistance."

She nodded, picking up a notebook and flipping through its pages. Angelo's handwriting was hurried, each line detailing troop movements, supply caches, and names of allies and informants. "He must have used this place to plan everything," she said. "It's like a time capsule."

Nico picked up a photograph from the table, his brow furrowing. "Elena, look at this."

The photograph showed a group of men and women standing in the cypress grove, their faces filled with determination. At the center stood Angelo, his arm around a young woman who wasn't Livia.

"Who is she?" Elena asked, her voice trembling.

"I don't know," Nico said. "But if she was important enough to be in Angelo's inner circle, she could be the key to understanding more."

A New Mystery

As they returned to the library with their findings, Elena's mind raced with questions. The woman in the photograph was unfamiliar, but something about her posture, the way she stood close to Angelo, felt significant.

"Do you think she was part of the resistance?" Nico asked, setting the photograph on the desk.

"She must have been," Elena replied. "But if she was that close to Angelo, why didn't Livia mention her in the journal?"

Nico leaned back in his chair, his expression thoughtful. "Maybe it was too painful. Or maybe there's more to their story than we've uncovered."

Elena nodded, her gaze fixed on the photograph. The villa had given her so much already—secrets, answers, and new questions. But now, it felt as though it was asking her to go further, to unravel the threads of a story that was still incomplete.

She picked up Angelo's notebook, her determination hardening. "We're not done yet."

Chapter 12: Shadows of Another Name

The library felt colder as Elena stared at the photograph spread out before her. Giulia Orlandi. The name hung in the air like an unanswered question. Her defiant gaze in the photograph, her closeness to Angelo—none of it made sense, and yet it felt like a missing piece of the puzzle.

"She had to matter to him," Elena said, her voice barely above a whisper. "But why didn't Livia mention her? There's no trace of her in the journals, no hint that she even existed."

Nico sat across from her, the glow of a lamp catching the lines of concern on his face. "What if Livia didn't know about her? Or worse—what if she knew but didn't want to?"

Elena shook her head. "Livia wrote everything. Every emotion, every secret. If Giulia was important—or dangerous—she would've been here." She gestured to the scattered journals and documents on the desk.

Her eyes returned to the letter Nico had discovered earlier, the faded ink trembling in her hands as she reread it.

Angelo,

The risks are growing. Every day, the shadows creep closer, and I fear for what lies ahead. But I have done what I must to protect you. Please understand—it was the only way. One day, I hope you will forgive me. Until then, trust that I remain loyal, even if my actions seem otherwise.

The words clawed at her, begging for answers. "What did she mean by that? Did she betray him? Protect him? Both?"

"It sounds like guilt," Nico said, leaning forward, his elbows resting on the desk. "But guilt for what? Giving up a name? Sabotaging a plan?"

"I don't know." Elena's voice cracked. She set the letter down and pressed her fingers to her temples. "This changes everything. If she betrayed Angelo, then the story I thought I knew—Livia's story—might not be the truth."

"And if she didn't?" Nico asked gently.

"Then maybe Angelo wasn't the man Livia thought he was either," Elena whispered, the thought chilling her.

They worked late into the night, pouring over Angelo's journals, Giulia's letter, and the stack of resistance documents they'd unearthed from the villa's underground chamber. Yet Giulia's name remained conspicuously absent, as though she'd been deliberately erased.

Elena stared at the photograph again, her eyes searching Giulia's face for answers. "She's a ghost," she said softly. "Either hidden or forgotten."

Nico stood, stretching his arms above his head. "If Angelo trusted her enough to keep her out of the records, it must've been for a reason. But that letter—he knew what she'd done."

Elena tightened her jaw. "He knew, but we don't. Not yet."

The sun had barely risen when they arrived at the Castelmare archives, tucked into the quiet corner of a cobblestone square. Elena carried Angelo's letter and the photograph as she approached the desk. An older man with round glasses perched on the tip of his nose looked up from a ledger.

"Good morning," she began, her voice steady despite her nerves. "I'm looking for information on someone who might have lived here during the war. Her name was Giulia Orlandi."

The man's brow furrowed. "Giulia, you say? There were many Giulias here during the war. Do you have a family name?"

Elena hesitated. "That is her family name."

"Ah," the man said, a glimmer of recognition sparking in his eyes. "Giulia Orlandi. Yes, I know of her."

Elena's breath caught. "You do?"

"She was part of the resistance," the clerk said, rising from his seat and gesturing for them to follow. "Her story... it's not without complications. But you may find what you're looking for in our records."

They followed him into a dimly lit room lined with shelves of faded documents. He selected a worn file and handed it to Elena. "This contains what we have. Be careful; some pages are delicate."

Elena opened the folder carefully, her pulse quickening as she sifted through names, notes, and faded photographs. And there, near the bottom, was another image of Giulia—her face unmistakable, though younger and more resolute.

"That's her," Elena murmured.

Nico leaned over her shoulder, nodding. "She looks... driven."

"She was," the clerk said from behind them. "Giulia Orlandi was known for her intelligence and boldness. She often worked closely with a man named Angelo Romano."

Elena's heart thudded. "What happened to her?"

The man hesitated, adjusting his glasses. "There are... mixed accounts. Some say she betrayed her comrades to the enemy.

Others claim she made a sacrifice to protect them. Whatever the truth, she disappeared near the end of the war. Her family's estate is just outside the village, though it's been abandoned for decades."

Elena closed the file slowly, her thoughts racing. "Thank you," she said, her voice steady but distant. "We'll check it out."

As they stepped back into the sunlight, Nico glanced at her, his expression serious. "We're going to the house, aren't we?"

Elena nodded, gripping the photograph tightly. "If Giulia's story is buried there, I'm going to find it."

Chapter 13: The House Beyond the Village

The road twisted like a ribbon through the hills, flanked by wildflowers swaying in the breeze. Each turn revealed another glimpse of the sea, a constant reminder of Castelmare's quiet pull. As the house came into view, its silhouette cast against the dark line of cypress trees, Elena felt her breath catch.

"This is where she disappeared," she said softly, gripping the steering wheel. The crumbling facade seemed to lean into the shadows of the grove, vines wrapping tightly around broken shutters and weathered stone walls, as though protecting the secrets within.

Nico's voice was calm beside her. "Are you sure you're ready?"

Elena nodded. "I have to be."

The iron gate creaked as they pushed it open, its rusted hinges protesting. Gravel crunched beneath their boots as they approached the house, the air heavy with the scent of damp earth and salt. The door hung slightly ajar, swinging inward with a low groan as Elena pushed it open.

Inside, the house was cloaked in darkness, her flashlight revealing layers of dust, toppled furniture, and walls cracked with age. She paused at a side table where a photograph, half-hidden beneath grime, caught her eye. Wiping it clean with her sleeve, she revealed a young woman standing proudly in front of the house. Giulia's sharp, confident gaze met hers, a defiance etched into her posture that felt as alive as the day the photograph was taken.

"She looks so certain of herself," Elena murmured, holding the frame toward Nico. "Like she still believed she could control what came next."

"She must have, at least for a while," Nico said, his eyes fixed on the image. "Until it all started to crumble."

They moved deeper into the house, the silence broken only by their footsteps and the occasional groan of the floorboards. In the study, Elena's flashlight caught a glint beneath a pile of yellowed papers. She crouched and pulled free a leather-bound journal, its cover embossed with the initials G.O..

Her breath caught as she opened it, the sharp handwriting inside speaking of a mind precise and driven. She began to read aloud, her voice low but steady.

"Angelo met me in the grove tonight. His faith in me is unwavering, but I wonder if it should be. The soldiers are closing in, and each decision I make feels heavier than the last. I betrayed one to save the others. Massimo. I've traded his life for Angelo's safety, but the cost feels unbearable."

Elena's hands trembled as she turned the page.

"The weight of what I've done is crushing. Angelo must never know. I fear it would destroy him—and what little remains of me."

She closed the journal, her chest tight. "She sacrificed a friend to save him. She lived with that guilt every day."

Nico leaned closer, his voice quiet. "But did Angelo ever find out?"

Elena didn't answer. Her fingers sifted through the desk drawers until they unearthed a wooden box sealed with a tarnished clasp. Inside, she found a stack of letters tied with a crimson ribbon. She untied it carefully and unfolded the top letter. Angelo's handwriting, raw and emotional, stretched across the page.

"Giulia,

I do not know the full extent of what you've done, but I cannot hate you. You acted as you thought best, even if it cost us dearly. I am leaving tonight, and I fear we will never meet again. Still, I carry no anger—only sorrow.

Yours always,

Angelo"

Elena's breath hitched. "He forgave her," she whispered. "Even though it tore them both apart."

"But she couldn't forgive herself," Nico said, his voice soft.

Elena folded the letter and placed it carefully back in the box, the weight of its words settling over her. She felt the years of guilt and love, tangled and unresolved, that had lingered in this house long after its inhabitants had gone.

In a corner of the study, they found a hidden door behind a warped bookshelf. Pushing it open revealed a small chamber, its walls lined with shelves crammed with documents, maps, and artifacts. A table in the center held scattered notes, faded photographs, and a delicate silver brooch.

Elena picked up a blueprint of the villa's underground chambers, annotations scrawled in Giulia's sharp hand marking supply routes and safe houses. "She was more than part of the resistance," she said quietly. "She was a leader. A strategist."

Nico examined a photograph on the table. Angelo and Giulia stood together, their faces solemn but defiant. "She wasn't just protecting him," he said. "She was protecting everything they were fighting for."

"And it cost her everything," Elena murmured.

As they left the house, the cypress trees swayed gently in the fading light, their whispers carrying a strange sense of peace. Elena held Giulia's journal and Angelo's letters close, her mind churning with all they had uncovered.

"She wasn't a villain," Elena said softly. "She was a woman who made impossible choices. Choices that saved lives, even as they broke her."

Nico nodded, his gaze steady. "And now her story can finally be told."

Elena looked back at the house one last time. Its cracked windows and sagging roofline no longer looked desolate. Instead, they stood as a monument to resilience, to sacrifice, and to a love that had endured the unthinkable.

Chapter 14: A Veil of Truth

The drive back to the villa was quiet, the setting sun casting long shadows across the hills. Elena's thoughts churned with everything they had uncovered in Giulia's house—the letters, the maps, and the notebook that revealed her secret life as a spy. Giulia Orlandi's story was more complex than she could have imagined, a web of loyalty and deception spun to protect the resistance and the man she loved.

Nico broke the silence. "Do you think Angelo ever forgave her?"

Elena glanced at him, her fingers tightening on the steering wheel. "I don't know. But he must have understood, at least. She risked everything for him—for the cause."

"And Livia?" Nico asked softly. "What would she have thought if she'd known?"

Elena's chest tightened. "I think it would have broken her. She loved Angelo so deeply, but knowing there was someone else who shared his trust—someone who risked her life for him—it would have changed everything."

The villa came into view, its silhouette stark against the deepening sky. Elena parked the car in the courtyard, the scent of jasmine and sea air enveloping them as they stepped out. The cypress trees swayed gently, their whispers seeming to echo the weight of the secrets they carried.

Piecing It Together

In the library, the artifacts from Giulia's house were spread across the desk: the letters, the maps, and her notebook. Elena sat in her chair, flipping through the pages again, each word deepening her understanding of the choices Giulia had made.

"She must have been terrified every day," Elena said, her voice barely above a whisper. "One mistake, and it all would have come crashing down."

Nico leaned against the desk, his arms crossed. "And yet, she kept going. She played both sides, knowing that if anyone discovered the truth, she'd lose everything."

Elena nodded, her gaze fixed on a particular passage in the notebook.

June 1943

The lies are becoming harder to maintain. They question me constantly, their eyes searching for cracks in my story. Angelo doesn't trust me anymore—I can see it in the way he looks at me. But I can't stop. If I stop, they'll find him. They'll find all of us.

Elena closed the notebook, her hands trembling. "She knew Angelo doubted her. He must have thought she was a traitor."

Nico frowned. "That would explain his letters to her—the warnings, the desperation. He didn't know what she was doing."

Elena looked up at him, her chest tight. "But she didn't stop. She kept going, even when he lost faith in her."

"Because she believed it was worth it," Nico said. "Even if it cost her everything."

A Letter Left Unread

As they sorted through the letters, Elena's fingers brushed against a folded piece of paper tucked into the back of the notebook. The edges were worn, the ink faded, but the handwriting was unmistakably Giulia's.

"This is different," Elena said, unfolding it carefully.

The letter was addressed to Angelo, but it was clear it had never been sent.

Angelo,

By the time you read this, I hope you will understand. I hope you will see that everything I've done was for you—for all of us. I never meant to hurt you, but I couldn't stand by and watch you be destroyed. If you hate me, so be it. But know that I have always loved you, even in the shadows.

Elena's breath caught as she read the final line aloud, her voice trembling. "She loved him."

Nico's expression softened. "She loved him enough to let him believe the worst about her."

Elena folded the letter carefully, placing it beside the others. "She didn't just save the resistance. She saved him. And he never knew."

A Glimpse of Forgiveness

That night, Elena sat alone in the courtyard, the cool air brushing against her skin as the cypress trees swayed overhead. The stars stretched endlessly above her, their light fractured and distant, yet steady.

Giulia's story weighed heavily on her. She thought of Livia, who had carried her own burdens for so many years, and of Angelo, who had lived with doubts that might never have been resolved. Their lives were intertwined, a tapestry of love, betrayal, and sacrifice.

Nico joined her, carrying a blanket. He draped it over her shoulders before settling into the chair beside her. "You've been quiet," he said gently.

"I've been thinking about Giulia," she replied. "About how much she gave up. Angelo never forgave her—not because he hated her, but because he didn't know the truth."

Nico nodded slowly. "Do you think that's why she wrote the letter? So he'd know someday?"

"Maybe," Elena said. "Or maybe it was just for herself. To put her feelings somewhere, even if no one else ever read them."

The wind rustled the leaves, carrying with it the faint scent of lavender from the garden. Elena closed her eyes, letting the sound wash over her. For the first time, she felt a sense of peace—not because the story was complete, but because she understood its weight.

"We'll tell her story," she said finally. "Giulia deserves to be remembered—not as a traitor, but as a woman who loved deeply and sacrificed everything."

Nico reached for her hand, his touch warm and steady. "And you're the one to do it."

Elena looked at him, her chest tightening with gratitude. "We'll do it together."

As the stars shimmered above them, the villa seemed to hum softly around her. The past was heavy, but it was no longer a burden. It was a gift—a legacy to carry forward, woven with threads of love, resilience, and truth.

Chapter 15: The Weight of Choices

Morning light seeped through the villa's tall windows, casting golden patterns across the library floor. Elena sat at the desk, her fingers brushing over Giulia's notebook. The edges were frayed, the leather soft and worn from years of use. Beside her lay the unsent letter to Angelo, its contents swirling in her mind like a tide that refused to settle.

"Everything she did was to protect him," Elena murmured, her voice barely above a whisper. "Even when it cost her his trust."

Nico stood by the window, the sunlight catching the lines of his profile. He turned toward her, his expression thoughtful. "And now it's up to you to make sure that truth doesn't get lost."

Elena nodded, her chest tightening. The weight of the past felt heavier today, as though the villa itself was asking her to carry its stories forward. She opened the notebook again, her gaze lingering on Giulia's words.

June 1943

The night is darker than usual. The enemy grows suspicious of my movements, and I can feel their eyes watching me. I want to run, to escape this web of lies I've spun, but I can't. Not yet. Angelo doesn't understand, but someday, I hope he will. If I fail, let this notebook be my confession.

Elena exhaled shakily, her fingers trembling as she closed the notebook. "She knew she might not survive," she said. "But she kept going. How do you live with that kind of fear?"

"By believing in something bigger than yourself," Nico replied. He crossed the room, resting his hand gently on her shoulder. "She believed she was saving Angelo, the resistance, maybe even the future."

"But it cost her everything," Elena whispered. "Her trust, her love, her life."

Nico crouched beside her, his gaze steady. "And now it's your job to make sure that cost wasn't for nothing."

A New Chapter

Elena spent the day pouring over the letters, journals, and artifacts from Giulia's house. Each fragment revealed another layer of the story, each word bringing her closer to understanding the woman who had loved Angelo enough to risk everything.

By evening, she had filled pages of her notebook with thoughts and connections, her handwriting looping wildly across the paper. The villa's walls seemed to hum with approval, as though it recognized her determination to uncover its secrets.

Nico appeared in the doorway, a tray of tea and biscuits in his hands. "You've been at this all day," he said, setting the tray down beside her. "Have you stopped to eat?"

Elena smiled faintly, reaching for the cup of tea. "Not really. I've been too caught up in all of this."

"And what have you found?" he asked, pulling up a chair beside her.

Elena opened her notebook, pointing to a passage she'd written earlier. "It's all starting to make sense now. Angelo wasn't just fighting for the resistance—he was fighting for Livia, for Giulia, for everyone who believed in something better. But he carried so much doubt, so much fear, that it blinded him to what was right in front of him."

"Giulia's love," Nico said softly.

Elena nodded. "And Livia's, too. They both loved him in different ways, and he tried to honor them both. But in the end, he lost them both because of the choices he had to make."

Nico reached for her hand, his touch warm and steady. "And now you're here to tell their story."

Elena smiled faintly, her chest tightening with gratitude. "I just hope I can do it justice."

The Call of the Villa

That night, Elena stepped onto the balcony overlooking the courtyard. The air was cool and crisp, the scent of jasmine and sea salt wrapping around her like an embrace. The cypress trees swayed gently in the breeze, their whispers carrying the weight of generations.

She leaned against the railing, her gaze fixed on the horizon where the sea met the sky. The villa's presence was palpable, its walls humming with life and memory. It felt alive, as though it were urging her forward, asking her to keep uncovering its secrets.

Nico joined her, a blanket draped over his arm. He wrapped it around her shoulders before leaning against the railing beside her. "What's next?" he asked.

Elena exhaled slowly, her breath visible in the cool night air. "There's still so much to uncover. Giulia's story is just one part of it. I need to know how it all connects—Livia, Angelo, Giulia, the resistance. The villa is the thread that ties it all together, but there are still pieces missing."

"And you're going to find them," Nico said, his voice filled with quiet certainty.

Elena glanced at him, a small smile tugging at her lips. "With your help, I will."

They stood together beneath the cypress sky, the stars scattered like diamonds above them. The villa seemed to watch over them, its presence both comforting and commanding. The past was calling, and Elena was ready to answer.

The villa's walls held more than just memories—they held stories waiting to be told. And Elena knew she was the one to tell them, to weave the threads of love, sacrifice, and resilience into something that would endure.

For the first time, she felt at peace—not because the work was done, but because she knew where it would lead.

Chapter 16: Beneath the Surface

The morning broke with a soft glow over Castelmare, the sun casting warm hues across the villa's timeworn stones. Elena stood in the courtyard, her fingers tracing the edges of Giulia's notebook. The quiet hum of the cypress trees surrounded her, their whispers urging her forward.

"Ready?" Nico's voice called from behind her, steady and reassuring.

She turned to see him standing near the arched doorway, a small spade in one hand and a flashlight tucked under his arm. The night before, they had combed through her notes, piecing together the remaining fragments of Giulia's story. A particular passage in her notebook had stood out, hinting at a final secret buried near the villa itself.

Elena nodded, her resolve firm. "Let's find out what she left behind."

Searching for the Past

The map they had sketched was rough but clear, leading them to a small, overgrown area near the villa's western wall. The space was bordered by wild lavender and olive trees, the scent mingling with the salty breeze from the sea. Elena crouched near a patch of earth, brushing aside the tangled grass.

"She wrote about this place," Elena said, her voice barely above a whisper. "It was where she and Angelo would meet in secret, away from the resistance and the eyes of the enemy."

Nico joined her, kneeling beside the marked spot. "If she left something here, she must have wanted it to stay hidden."

They began to dig, the spade slicing into the earth with soft, rhythmic movements. The soil was damp and heavy, clinging to their hands as they worked. Minutes passed in silence, the only sounds the distant crash of waves and the rustling of leaves.

Finally, Nico's spade hit something solid. "Here," he said, brushing away the loose dirt. "There's something here."

Elena leaned forward, her heart pounding as she unearthed a small wooden box. The edges were worn, the wood darkened with age, but the clasp was intact. She opened it carefully, her breath catching as she saw the contents.

Inside was a delicate brooch in the shape of a cypress tree, its silver surface tarnished but still gleaming. Beneath it lay a bundle of papers, tied with a faded ribbon. Elena's fingers trembled as she untied the ribbon and unfolded the first page.

Angelo,

If you are reading this, then the war is over, and I am gone. I don't know what will remain of us, of what we fought for, but I want you to know the truth. I never betrayed you—not in the way you feared. Everything I did was for the resistance, for you, for the people we hoped to save. This brooch belonged to my mother. It was the last thing she gave me before she died, and now I give it to you. Keep it, or bury it. But let it remind you that even in the darkest moments, there was love.

Giulia

Elena's voice faltered as she read the words aloud, her throat tightening with emotion. She handed the letter to Nico, her chest heavy with the weight of Giulia's final message.

"She wanted him to know the truth," Elena said. "Even if it was too late."

Nico nodded, his gaze fixed on the brooch. "And she left this as a symbol—of her love, her loyalty."

Elena carefully placed the letter and brooch back in the box, her hands trembling. The discovery felt monumental, as though they had uncovered not just a piece of history but a piece of Giulia herself.

The Villa's Response

Back inside the villa, Elena sat at the library desk, the box resting before her. The sunlight streamed through the windows, casting long shadows across the room. She traced the edges of the brooch with her fingers, its intricate design both delicate and strong.

"This changes everything," she said softly.

Nico sat across from her, his expression thoughtful. "How so?"

Elena glanced at him, her eyes filled with determination. "Giulia's story isn't just about sacrifice—it's about redemption. She wasn't perfect, but she did everything she could to protect the people she loved. Her story needs to be told, alongside Livia's and Angelo's."

Nico smiled faintly, his gaze steady. "Then that's what we'll do."

Elena picked up her pen, her notebook open to a fresh page. She began writing, the words flowing effortlessly as she wove Giulia's story into the tapestry of the villa's history. The brooch sat beside her, a quiet reminder of the woman who had loved in the shadows and fought in the light.

A Visitor Returns

Later that evening, as the sky deepened into twilight, the sound of a car pulling into the courtyard broke the villa's tranquil silence. Elena and Nico stepped outside, their curiosity piqued. A sleek black sedan had parked near the fountain, and Pietro Romano emerged, his expression grave.

"I heard you found something," he said, his voice low.

Elena nodded, gesturing for him to follow her into the library. Once inside, she showed him the box and its contents, explaining their discovery near the western wall.

Pietro picked up the brooch, his fingers tracing its intricate design. "This belonged to her," he said softly. "My grandmother spoke of it once, but she never told me what happened to it."

Elena's breath caught. "Your grandmother?"

Pietro nodded, his gaze meeting hers. "Giulia was my grandmother. My father was her son, born years after the war. She rarely spoke of those days, but when she did, it was always with a mix of pride and sorrow."

Elena's chest tightened as the weight of the connection settled over her. "She left this for Angelo, but it was never found."

Pietro smiled faintly. "Until now. Thank you for bringing this part of her story back to life."

Threads Woven Together

As night fell, the three of them sat in the library, sharing stories and piecing together the fragments of Giulia's life. Pietro's memories of his grandmother added new layers to the narrative, painting a picture of a woman who had loved deeply, sacrificed greatly, and carried her secrets to the grave.

By the time Pietro left, the villa felt different—lighter, as though it had released a burden it had carried for decades.

Elena stood in the courtyard, the cypress trees swaying gently above her.

"She gave so much," Elena said, her voice quiet. "And now, finally, her story is being told."

Nico stepped beside her, his hand brushing hers. "And you're the one telling it."

Elena smiled faintly, her chest filled with a sense of purpose. The villa's whispers seemed softer now, no longer demanding but grateful. The past was coming to light, and with it, the promise of something new.

Beneath the cypress sky, Elena felt the weight of the villa's legacy settle over her—and for the first time, it felt like a gift.

Chapter 17: A Tangled Legacy

The morning sun poured over Castelmare, casting a warm glow on the villa's facade. Inside, Elena stood in the library, the delicate brooch resting in her palm. Giulia's words echoed in her mind—words of love, loyalty, and sacrifice. They had uncovered so much, yet the story still felt incomplete.

She looked up as Nico entered, carrying two steaming cups of coffee. "You've been staring at that thing all morning," he said, setting a cup on the desk.

"It's not just a thing," Elena replied softly. "It's her truth. A symbol of everything she gave up—and everything she believed in."

Nico pulled out a chair and sat across from her. "Do you think Angelo ever saw it?"

Elena shook her head. "No. If he had, it might have changed everything."

Nico leaned forward, his gaze steady. "Then maybe it's time to show it to someone who can help us understand."

Elena frowned. "Who?"

Nico paused before answering. "The archives clerk mentioned there were others who might remember Giulia—or her connection to Angelo. We should talk to them."

Voices of the Past

The village square bustled with life, the scent of fresh bread and roasted coffee filling the air as Elena and Nico made their way to the archives. The clerk greeted them warmly, his glasses perched precariously on his nose.

"You're back," he said, his voice tinged with curiosity. "Have you found more?"

Elena nodded, setting the brooch on the counter. "We found this near the villa. It belonged to Giulia Orlandi."

The clerk's eyes widened as he picked up the brooch, turning it over in his hands. "Ah, yes. I've seen this design before. The Orlandi family was known for their craftsmanship—this was likely made by her father."

"Do you know anyone who might have known her?" Elena asked. "Someone who could tell us more about her life after the war?"

The clerk thought for a moment before nodding. "There is one person. An old woman who lives near the church. She was a friend of Giulia's mother—a child during the war, but she might remember something."

The house near the church was small but well-kept, its pale yellow walls adorned with blooming geraniums. Elena knocked softly on the wooden door, her heart racing as the sound of shuffling footsteps approached.

The door opened to reveal a petite woman with silver hair and kind, dark eyes. "Yes?" she asked, her voice warm but cautious.

"Are you Signora Fontana?" Elena asked.

The woman nodded. "I am. And you are?"

"My name is Elena Marconi. I'm trying to piece together a story—about Giulia Orlandi."

Signora Fontana's expression softened at the name, a faint smile tugging at her lips. "Ah, Giulia. I remember her well. Come in."

Recollections

The interior of Signora Fontana's house was cozy, the scent of lavender and aged wood filling the air. She gestured for Elena and Nico to sit at a small table, then disappeared into the kitchen, returning moments later with a tray of tea and biscuits.

"Giulia was a kind soul," Signora Fontana began, settling into her chair. "But she carried a heaviness with her, even after the war."

Elena leaned forward. "Do you know what happened to her? After the resistance?"

Signora Fontana sighed, her gaze distant. "She stayed here, in Castelmare, for a while. But the war had changed her. She rarely spoke of what she had done, though there were whispers—rumors that she had betrayed the resistance."

"She didn't," Elena said quickly. "We found her letters, her notebook. She was working as a spy, feeding false information to the enemy to protect Angelo and the others."

Signora Fontana's eyes widened, tears brimming. "That explains so much. She was ostracized after the war—people believed she had sold out her friends. Even Angelo... he left without ever speaking to her again."

Elena's chest tightened. "She lived with that her entire life?"

Signora Fontana nodded sadly. "She stayed for a few years, but eventually, she left Castelmare. No one knew where she went. Some said she started a new life far away, where no one knew her name."

A Lingering Question

Back at the villa, Elena sat in the courtyard, the brooch resting on the table before her. The weight of Giulia's story pressed heavily on her heart. She thought of Livia, Angelo, and the countless others who had carried burdens that time could not erase.

"She was forgotten," Elena said as Nico joined her, his presence as steadying as always. "Even though she gave everything, the world remembered her as a traitor."

"But you've found the truth," Nico said gently. "And you're going to make sure she's remembered for who she really was."

Elena nodded, her jaw tightening with resolve. "I owe her that much."

A Chance Discovery

That night, as Elena sorted through the papers they had collected, she noticed something she had missed before: a small slip of paper tucked into the lining of Giulia's notebook. The ink was faded, but the message was clear.

To whoever finds this: I did not do this for recognition or thanks. I did it because it was the only way to protect the people I loved. If my name is forgotten, so be it. But let the truth live on.

Elena's breath caught as she read the words aloud, her voice trembling. She looked at Nico, her chest tight with emotion. "She knew no one would believe her. But she still wanted the truth to matter."

"And now it does," Nico said softly. "Because of you."

Elena smiled faintly, her resolve hardening. The villa's whispers seemed louder now, not demanding but encouraging.

The past was waiting, and she was ready to uncover every last piece.

As the stars stretched across the sky, Elena felt a quiet determination settle over her. Giulia's story would not be forgotten. Neither would Livia's or Angelo's. Beneath the cypress sky, their legacies would live on—and so would hers.

Chapter 18: Unraveling the Web

The morning broke with a haze of golden light spilling across the hills, bathing the villa in warmth. Elena sat in the library, the brooch resting beside her on the desk. Before her lay scattered papers: letters from Giulia, fragments of Livia's journals, and Angelo's resistance maps. The pieces were all there, yet the story remained incomplete.

Nico entered, carrying a tray of coffee and fresh pastries. He set it down without a word, pulling up a chair beside her.

"You've been up early," he said.

"I couldn't sleep," Elena replied, her voice low. "There's something I'm missing—something Giulia wrote about the enemy's movements, and Angelo's maps... It's like they don't match."

"Don't match how?" Nico asked, leaning closer.

Elena pointed to a cluster of markings on the map. "Angelo tracked troop positions here, near the eastern hills. But Giulia's notes show a different pattern, one that circles Castelmare. It's almost as if..."

Nico raised an eyebrow. "As if she was keeping them away?"

Elena nodded, her pulse quickening. "She wasn't just feeding false information—she was redirecting them, keeping them from finding the resistance hideouts."

"And Angelo never knew?" Nico asked.

"He didn't trust her," Elena said, her voice heavy with sadness. "He thought she was playing both sides. But she was protecting them the whole time."

The Hidden Vault

As the morning unfolded, Elena and Nico pored over the documents, tracing the movements Giulia had recorded. The patterns were clear now: her actions had shielded Castelmare from invasion, her deceptions leading the enemy into wild goose chases across the hills. But the question lingered—how had she maintained the ruse for so long?

"Giulia must have had help," Elena said, pacing the library. "She couldn't have done this alone."

"Then we need to find out who," Nico replied.

Their search led them to the northern wing of the villa, to a room they had yet to explore. The air was cool and stale as they pushed open the heavy door, revealing a narrow chamber lined with shelves. Books and artifacts filled the space, their age evident in the layers of dust that coated them.

Near the back of the room, Nico spotted a small cabinet. "Here," he said, tugging at its latch.

The cabinet door creaked open, revealing a bundle of documents tied with a crimson ribbon. Elena's breath caught as she untied it, her fingers trembling as she unfolded the top sheet.

It was a ledger, filled with names, dates, and locations. The handwriting was unfamiliar, but the content was clear: it was a record of communications, a web of contacts that spanned the region.

"These were Giulia's allies," Elena whispered. "She wasn't working alone."

A New Connection

One name stood out among the entries: Marcello Bonetti. Elena's heart raced as she scanned the ledger for more information. His name appeared repeatedly, linked to messages delivered and resources secured.

"Marcello," she murmured. "He must have been her contact here in Castelmare."

"Do you think he's still alive?" Nico asked.

"If he is, he might have answers," Elena replied.

They returned to the archives, hoping the clerk could point them toward Marcello. The older man nodded thoughtfully at the name. "Marcello Bonetti? Yes, he's still here. Lives on the outskirts of town, near the old olive grove. He keeps to himself these days."

A Meeting with Marcello

The olive grove was quiet, the trees swaying gently in the breeze. Elena and Nico approached a modest stone house nestled among the rows, its windows shuttered against the sun. Elena knocked softly, her heart pounding.

The door opened to reveal an older man with sharp eyes and a weathered face. He studied them for a moment before speaking. "Who are you?"

"My name is Elena Marconi," she began. "I'm trying to learn about Giulia Orlandi—and her work during the war."

At the mention of Giulia's name, Marcello's expression shifted, his gaze narrowing. "Why now? Why, after all these years, do you want to know about her?"

"She deserves to be remembered for what she truly did," Elena said. "Not as a traitor, but as someone who saved the resistance—and Castelmare."

Marcello's jaw tightened. He stepped aside, gesturing for them to enter. "Come in."

The Untold Story

Inside, the house was simple, its walls lined with books and photographs. Marcello motioned for them to sit before taking a chair opposite them. His gaze was distant as he began to speak.

"Giulia was the bravest person I ever knew," he said. "She worked in the shadows, keeping the enemy off our trail. Every move she made was calculated, every risk deliberate."

"She mentioned you in her ledger," Elena said. "You helped her?"

Marcello nodded. "I was her courier. I carried her messages, smuggled supplies. She couldn't risk being seen in the open, so I became her link to the outside world."

"Did Angelo know?" Nico asked.

Marcello's expression darkened. "No. He didn't trust her. He thought she was feeding information to the enemy. When the rumors started, he distanced himself from her. She never stopped caring for him, though—not for a second."

Elena felt a lump rise in her throat. "Why didn't she defend herself?"

"Because it didn't matter to her," Marcello said. "All that mattered was the resistance—and Angelo's safety."

He reached for a small box on the shelf, pulling out a faded photograph. It showed Giulia standing beside Marcello, her eyes filled with quiet determination. "She gave everything for us. And she died carrying the weight of a betrayal she didn't commit."

The Weight of Truth

Back at the villa, Elena sat in the courtyard, Marcello's words echoing in her mind. Giulia's sacrifices had saved countless lives, yet she had been remembered as a traitor. The injustice of it burned in Elena's chest, filling her with a renewed sense of purpose.

Nico joined her, his presence steadying. "You're going to write about her, aren't you?"

Elena nodded, her voice firm. "She deserves that much—and more."

As the cypress trees swayed above them, Elena felt the weight of the villa's legacy settle over her once more. The past was tangled, its threads woven with pain and sacrifice. But in those threads lay a story of resilience and love, one that deserved to be told.

Under the evening sky, Elena made a silent promise: Giulia's name would be remembered, not as a shadow of doubt, but as a beacon of courage.

Chapter 19: Threads of Redemption

The evening sun cast long shadows across the courtyard, its light pooling in soft golds and ambers. Elena stood near the fountain, her thoughts swirling with everything Marcello had told her. The image of Giulia—misunderstood, sacrificing everything for a cause she believed in—burned in her mind. A breeze stirred the cypress trees above, their gentle rustling like a whisper urging her forward.

Nico approached, his hands tucked into his pockets, his expression thoughtful. "You've been quiet since we got back."

Elena glanced at him, her brow furrowed. "I can't stop thinking about what Marcello said. Angelo never knew the truth. He lived believing Giulia betrayed him."

Nico stepped closer, his voice steady. "But now you know. And you can make sure the world knows, too."

Elena nodded, her resolve hardening. "She gave up everything, Nico. Her name, her reputation, even her life. And for what? So people could call her a traitor?"

"She gave it up because she believed it was worth it," Nico said gently. "And you're here to prove she was right."

The Past Unearthed

The library was quiet, bathed in the golden hues of twilight as Elena and Nico returned to their research. Giulia's ledger sat open on the desk, her delicate handwriting filling its pages. Beside it lay Livia's journal and Angelo's resistance maps, their details now illuminated by the truths Marcello had revealed.

"She was protecting him the entire time," Elena murmured, her fingers tracing the edge of the ledger. "Even when he turned away from her."

Nico nodded. "And she did it knowing he might never forgive her."

Elena's gaze shifted to Livia's journal, its familiar lines etched with emotion. "And Livia—she never knew about any of this. She only knew the Angelo who doubted Giulia."

"Maybe it's better that way," Nico said. "Livia loved him for who he was with her, not for the doubts and struggles he carried."

Elena's jaw tightened. "But it's not fair. Giulia deserves to be remembered for what she truly was: a hero."

She picked up a blank notebook, her hand hovering over the page. The brooch lay nearby, its silver surface glinting in the fading light. "If I'm going to tell her story, I need to start now."

Nico watched her for a moment before placing a hand on her shoulder. "Then let's do it."

A Letter to the Future

Elena's pen moved across the page, her thoughts spilling into words. She began with the brooch, its delicate design a symbol of Giulia's sacrifices. From there, she wove the story of Giulia's work in the resistance, her love for Angelo, and the choices that had defined her life.

The room grew darker as the sun dipped below the horizon, and Nico lit the lamps, their soft glow filling the space. Hours passed, the sound of Elena's pen scratching against paper the only noise.

Finally, she paused, her chest tightening as she reread her words. "It's not enough," she said softly. "There's still more to tell."

"There always will be," Nico replied. "But this is a start. And it's beautiful."

Elena looked at him, her heart swelling with gratitude. "Thank you. For being here—for helping me."

Nico smiled faintly, his voice warm. "You don't have to thank me. This is your story, Elena. I'm just here to make sure you don't forget that."

The Village Responds

A week later, Elena and Nico returned to Castelmare with their findings. They shared Giulia's ledger, her letters, and the truth of her sacrifices with the local archives. The response was immediate: whispers of her heroism spread through the village, replacing the long-held rumors of betrayal.

At the village square, an impromptu gathering formed as neighbors shared stories and memories of the resistance. Pietro Romano stood near the center, his voice steady as he recounted Angelo's courage and Giulia's quiet strength.

"She was misunderstood," Pietro said. "But now, thanks to Elena, we can finally honor her for what she was."

Elena stood at the edge of the crowd, her heart heavy but full. The brooch rested in her pocket, its weight a constant reminder of the legacy she carried.

Nico leaned toward her, his voice low. "You did this."

"We did this," she corrected, her gaze sweeping over the crowd. "Giulia deserves to be remembered—not as a shadow, but as a light."

A Step Forward

That evening, as the villa's lights flickered against the night, Elena stood on the balcony overlooking the cliffs. The sea stretched endlessly before her, its waves crashing softly against the rocks below.

Nico joined her, his presence a steady comfort. "How does it feel?" he asked.

Elena took a deep breath, the salty air filling her lungs. "It feels like we've taken the first step. But there's still so much more to uncover."

Nico smiled faintly. "Then we keep going."

She looked at him, her chest tightening with gratitude. "We?"

He nodded. "You didn't think I was going to leave you now, did you?"

Elena laughed softly, the sound carrying on the breeze. "No. I suppose not."

As the stars stretched across the sky, Elena felt a sense of peace settle over her. The villa's whispers seemed softer now, their weight no longer a burden but a promise. Giulia's story was just the beginning. Beneath the cypress sky, there were still countless threads to weave—and Elena was ready to find them all.

Chapter 20: Beneath the Cypress Sky

The dawn brought a stillness to Castelmare, the early light stretching across the villa's walls like a gentle caress. Elena stood in the courtyard, her hands brushing the stone fountain's edge. The brooch rested in her pocket, its presence a constant reminder of the journey she had undertaken. The villa's whispers seemed quieter now, as though it were finally at peace with the truths she had uncovered.

Nico approached from the library, carrying a small stack of papers bound with twine. "I've organized the first draft," he said, offering her the bundle. "Everything we've pieced together—Giulia's story, Angelo's letters, Livia's journals. It's all here."

Elena accepted the papers, her chest tightening with emotion. "It feels so small," she said, her voice soft. "After everything they endured, everything they gave up... this feels like so little."

Nico shook his head. "It's not small. It's everything. You've given their sacrifices meaning. Their voices will be heard."

She looked up at him, the weight of his words settling over her. "Thank you," she said. "For believing in me."

"I always have," he replied, his smile warm.

The Gathering

Later that day, Elena and Nico hosted a small gathering at the villa. Neighbors from Castelmare arrived, along with historians and Pietro Romano, who brought photographs and keepsakes from his family's archives. The villa seemed to hum with energy as its halls filled with voices, the air alive with stories of the past.

Elena stood in the center of the library, the brooch glinting softly on the desk beside her. She held a notebook in her hands, its pages filled with the story she had worked so hard to piece together.

"Thank you all for being here," she began, her voice steady despite the emotions welling inside her. "This villa has held so many secrets, so many stories waiting to be told. Today, we honor one of those stories—the story of Giulia Orlandi."

The room grew quiet, the weight of her words settling over the crowd. Pietro stepped forward, his expression solemn. "Giulia was my grandmother. For years, her name was spoken in whispers, often with judgment and misunderstanding. But thanks to Elena, we now know the truth: she was a hero."

Elena's chest swelled with pride and gratitude as the room erupted in quiet applause. The villa seemed to echo the sentiment, its walls alive with the sound of appreciation.

A Moment of Reflection

As the evening wore on, the gathering slowly dispersed, leaving the villa in a serene stillness. Elena walked through the empty halls, her footsteps echoing softly. The brooch rested in her palm, its silver surface cool against her skin.

She paused beneath the portrait of Livia in the great hall, her gaze meeting her grandmother's. "You carried so much," she murmured. "More than anyone should have to. But you weren't alone. Angelo, Giulia—they were part of your story, just as you were part of theirs."

The air seemed to shift, a gentle breeze brushing through the hall despite the stillness outside. Elena smiled faintly, feeling the villa's quiet approval.

A Promise Made

That night, Elena and Nico sat on the balcony overlooking the sea. The stars stretched endlessly above them, their light mirrored in the dark waves below. Elena held the brooch in her hand, its weight grounding her.

"What happens now?" Nico asked.

Elena glanced at him, her gaze steady. "I finish the story. Not just for Giulia, but for Livia, Angelo, and everyone who gave so much for something bigger than themselves. Their stories deserve to be told."

"And what about your story?" he asked, his voice soft.

She smiled, her heart swelling. "It's still being written."

Nico reached for her hand, his touch warm and reassuring. "Then let's make it a good one."

Elena leaned against him, her chest light despite the weight of the past. Beneath the cypress sky, the villa had given her so much—truth, purpose, and a connection to something greater. As the waves crashed softly below, she felt a quiet peace settle over her.

The story was far from over, but for the first time, she felt ready for whatever came next. Beneath the stars and the gentle whispers of the cypress trees, Elena knew she was exactly where she was meant to be.

Chapter 21: Echoes of the Resistance

The morning brought a crisp, salty breeze from the sea, and the villa's stones glowed warmly in the sunlight. Elena sat at the library desk, her pen poised over a blank page. The previous evening's gathering had left her with a renewed sense of purpose, but the weight of the story she was writing still pressed heavily on her.

Nico entered the room carrying two mugs of steaming coffee. "You didn't sleep much," he said, placing one beside her.

She glanced up, offering him a faint smile. "Too much on my mind."

He pulled a chair closer, sitting beside her. "What's the next piece?"

Elena tapped the pen against her notebook. "The resistance. I need to understand what it meant to them—not just the fight, but the sacrifices, the betrayals. Giulia's story was only one thread in a much larger tapestry."

"You think there are others who can help?" Nico asked.

She nodded. "Marcello might know more. And the archives clerk mentioned something about old resistance records stored in the village church."

"Then we go there," Nico said, his tone resolute.

A Sacred Vault

The village church stood on a gentle rise, its stone walls weathered by centuries of wind and sun. Inside, the air was cool and still, carrying the faint scent of incense. Elena and Nico approached the priest, an older man with a kind face and a steady voice.

"Father Matteo," Elena began, "we're looking for information about the resistance during the war. We were told there might be records stored here."

The priest studied them for a moment before nodding. "Follow me."

He led them to a small, locked door near the back of the church. Producing an old key, he turned the lock, and the door creaked open to reveal a dimly lit room lined with shelves. Papers, photographs, and bound ledgers filled the space, their presence a quiet testament to the lives and struggles of the past.

"These records were kept by the resistance themselves," Father Matteo explained. "After the war, they were brought here for safekeeping. Not many have asked about them in years."

Elena's heart quickened as she stepped inside, her fingers brushing the edges of the papers. "Thank you," she said. "This means more than I can say."

Secrets Unearthed

Elena and Nico spent hours sifting through the records. They uncovered troop movements, supply routes, and names of those who had fought and fallen. Giulia's name appeared several times, always tied to critical moments: the diversion of enemy forces, the smuggling of supplies, the protection of key resistance members.

"She was everywhere," Nico said, marveling at the scope of her involvement. "It's like she was holding the entire operation together."

Elena nodded, her chest tight with emotion. "And yet, she was the one they doubted."

Among the papers, Elena found a letter addressed to Angelo, unsigned but unmistakably written by a resistance leader.

Angelo,

You have your doubts about Giulia, but I ask you to look beyond the rumors. She has done more for this cause than most will ever know. If we lose her, we lose a key piece of our strength. Trust is difficult in times like these, but she has earned mine—and yours as well.

Elena read the words aloud, her voice trembling. "Even the leaders believed in her. Why couldn't Angelo see it?"

"Fear does strange things," Nico said. "He probably thought it was safer to assume the worst than risk everything."

"But he was wrong," Elena said firmly. "And Giulia paid the price."

A New Discovery

As they were preparing to leave, Elena noticed a sealed envelope tucked inside one of the ledgers. The paper was brittle, the ink faint, but the handwriting was unmistakable—it was Livia's.

"Livia?" Nico asked, peering over her shoulder.

Elena nodded, her hands trembling as she carefully opened the envelope. Inside was a single page, written in her grandmother's elegant script.

To whoever finds this,

The villa has seen so much—love, loss, betrayal, and hope. It holds our secrets, but it also holds our strength. I was never brave enough to tell this story myself, but I hope someone will. Giulia, Angelo, and all the others—they deserve to be remembered not for their flaws, but for their courage. Whoever you are, thank you for listening to the whispers of these walls. And thank you for telling the truth.

Livia

Tears blurred Elena's vision as she read the letter aloud. The words felt like a blessing, a permission to carry the story forward.

"She knew this would happen," Elena said softly. "She trusted the villa to keep these stories safe until someone was ready to tell them."

"And now it's you," Nico said, his voice steady. "You're the one she was waiting for."

Elena folded the letter carefully, her chest swelling with emotion. The weight of the past no longer felt like a burden—it felt like a calling.

Back at the Villa

That evening, Elena sat at her desk, Livia's letter resting beside her. The villa was quiet, its whispers soft and soothing. She picked up her pen, her heart full as she began to write.

Beneath the cypress sky, where the sea meets the cliffs of Castelmare, stories of love and sacrifice have endured for generations. This is one of those stories—the story of a villa that held its secrets until the world was ready to hear them, and of the people who gave everything to protect what mattered most.

The words flowed easily now, each one carrying the weight of truth and memory. Elena wrote late into the night, the villa's presence a steady companion. For the first time, she felt truly connected—not just to Livia, Angelo, and Giulia, but to the countless others who had walked these halls, leaving their mark on its stones.

As the stars glittered above and the cypress trees swayed gently in the breeze, Elena felt a quiet peace settle over her. The villa's story was hers to tell, and she was ready to tell it

Chapter 22: The Forgotten Names

The following morning dawned bright and clear, the villa bathed in golden light. Elena stood at the library desk, staring at the collection of documents and artifacts she had spent weeks uncovering. Each piece of paper, every artifact, held a fragment of a story—a name, a place, a moment—but they also hinted at the many lives that had been part of the resistance.

She picked up a photograph of a group of resistance members, their faces youthful yet marked by determination. Giulia stood near the center, her expression resolute, while Angelo lingered on the edge, his eyes shadowed by doubt. There were others in the photo, faces Elena didn't recognize.

"We've focused so much on Angelo and Giulia," she said aloud, turning to Nico, who leaned against the doorway with a mug of coffee. "But they weren't the only ones. Look at all these people—they risked everything, too. How many of their stories have been lost?"

Nico took a sip of coffee, his gaze thoughtful. "You're right. If the villa's walls could talk, it would be about more than just Angelo and Giulia. There's a bigger story here."

Elena nodded, her chest tightening with resolve. "Then let's find it."

A Search for Names

The archives were quiet when they arrived, the scent of aged paper and wood filling the air. The clerk greeted them warmly, his curiosity evident as they explained their new focus.

"I want to know about the others," Elena said, showing him the photograph. "Their names, their roles in the resistance—anything you have."

The clerk adjusted his glasses, studying the image. "This will take time. Many of the records from that era were fragmented, and not all the names were documented."

"We're willing to look through whatever you have," Nico said. "Anything that might help."

The clerk led them to a long table stacked with old boxes and binders. "These are what we have on the resistance members who operated near Castelmare. It's incomplete, but perhaps it will give you something."

Piecing the Puzzle

For hours, Elena and Nico sifted through the records, piecing together names, roles, and connections. Some were listed as couriers or informants, while others were noted as fighters or strategists. Many names appeared only once, their contributions lost to time.

"Here," Elena said, pointing to a document. "This mentions a Carlo Venturi. He was listed as one of the primary contacts for supply lines."

Nico scanned the paper. "And here's a record of a Lucia Ferrante. She was involved in coordinating safe houses."

Elena added the names to her notebook, her list growing steadily. Each name felt like a small victory, a piece of the resistance brought back to light. Yet with every discovery came the realization of how much had been forgotten.

"These people gave everything," Elena said softly, her voice tinged with sadness. "But history barely remembers them."

"That's why we're doing this," Nico reminded her. "To make sure they're not forgotten."

A Link to the Present

As they continued their search, one name stood out: Matteo Ferrante. He was listed as a resistance fighter who had worked closely with Angelo. A note beside his name indicated that he had survived the war and remained in Castelmare for many years.

"Matteo Ferrante," Elena murmured. "He must be related to Lucia."

Nico leaned back in his chair. "If he stayed here after the war, maybe someone in the village remembers him."

They returned to the clerk, who nodded at the name. "Matteo Ferrante was well-known in Castelmare after the war. He passed away some years ago, but his grandson still lives here. I believe he owns a small café near the market."

A Conversation at the Café

The café was a charming, sunlit space nestled in a quiet corner of the market square. The scent of freshly brewed coffee and baked pastries filled the air as Elena and Nico approached the counter. A young man with dark hair and a warm smile greeted them.

"Welcome," he said. "What can I get for you?"

"Are you Lorenzo Ferrante?" Elena asked.

The man nodded, his smile faltering slightly. "I am. Why do you ask?"

"I'm Elena Marconi," she said. "I'm writing about the resistance during the war, and I've come across your grandfather's name. I was hoping you could tell me about him."

Lorenzo's expression softened. "Nonno Matteo... He didn't talk much about the war, but when he did, it was with pride. He always said he fought for the people he loved—for Castelmare."

"Do you know anything about the group he worked with?" Nico asked. "People like Angelo Romano or Giulia Orlandi?"

Lorenzo's brow furrowed. "He mentioned Angelo a few times, always with respect. Giulia... I remember he called her brave. Said she was misunderstood by many but never by him."

Elena's chest tightened. "Did he leave anything behind? Letters, journals—anything that might tell us more about that time?"

Lorenzo nodded. "There's an old trunk in the back room. It's mostly family mementos, but you're welcome to look."

The Trunk's Secrets

The trunk was filled with photographs, letters, and keepsakes from Matteo's life. Among them, Elena found a small, leather-bound notebook. The pages were filled with Matteo's careful handwriting, recounting his experiences during the war.

One entry caught her attention:

April 1944

Giulia Orlandi saved us today. The enemy was closing in, but her quick thinking diverted them, giving us time to escape. Angelo doesn't trust her, but he's wrong. She's as loyal as they come. I just hope she survives this war. The world will need people like her when it's over.

Elena's hands trembled as she read the words. "He believed in her," she said softly. "Even when Angelo didn't."

Nico placed a hand on her shoulder. "It's another piece of her truth. Another voice telling her story."

Elena carefully closed the notebook, her heart full yet heavy. "We're not just telling Giulia's story anymore," she said. "We're telling all of theirs."

Carrying the Names Forward

That night, back at the villa, Elena sat in the courtyard with her growing list of names. Each one felt like a small victory, a life remembered, a legacy restored. The cypress trees swayed gently above her, their whispers carrying the weight of the past.

Nico joined her, a bottle of wine and two glasses in hand. "How's it going?" he asked, pouring them each a glass.

Elena smiled faintly. "It's overwhelming, but it feels right. These people—they deserve to be known. They fought for something bigger than themselves, and their stories need to be told."

"To the resistance," Nico said, raising his glass.

"To the resistance," Elena echoed, her voice filled with quiet determination.

As the stars stretched across the night sky, Elena felt the villa's presence envelop her like an embrace. The past was vast, its threads tangled and complex, but she was ready to untangle them—one name, one story at a time.

Chapter 23: Weaving the Stories

The dawn was soft, with golden rays filtering through the villa's arched windows. Elena sat at her desk in the library, the collection of names and stories spread before her. Each name carried weight, each story a reminder of the sacrifices made during the war. The villa felt alive this morning, its whispers urging her forward.

Nico entered, carrying a tray with coffee and a plate of biscuits. "You've been up for hours," he said, setting the tray down.

"I couldn't stop thinking about the list," Elena replied. "Each name feels like a thread, and it's up to me to weave them into something whole."

Nico leaned on the desk, his gaze steady. "Where do you start?"

"With the truth," Elena said simply.

A Hidden Connection

As she sifted through Matteo Ferrante's notebook again, a passage caught Elena's attention. It described a resistance meeting held at the villa, one that included names from her growing list—names like Lucia Ferrante, Marcello Bonetti, and even Angelo Romano.

"They met here," she said aloud, her voice filled with awe. "The villa wasn't just a home—it was a sanctuary for the resistance."

Nico's brow furrowed. "That explains why so many of the documents we've found were hidden here. This place was more than just a shelter—it was a headquarters."

Elena nodded, her mind racing. "And Livia... she must have known. Even if she wasn't directly involved, she was part of this."

Turning back to Livia's journal, Elena found an entry that confirmed her suspicions:

March 1944

The meetings have become more frequent. Angelo is always tense, always looking over his shoulder. I hear whispers of plans, of movements and betrayals. I stay out of the way, but the villa feels heavier now, as though it knows it is holding secrets that could cost lives.

Elena's chest tightened as she read the words. "She was afraid, but she never stopped supporting Angelo."

"She loved him," Nico said softly. "Enough to carry his burdens, even if she didn't understand them."

Elena closed the journal carefully, her resolve hardening. "I need to tell the story of this villa—not just as a home, but as a cornerstone of the resistance."

An Unexpected Visitor

As the morning stretched into afternoon, the sound of a car pulling into the courtyard drew Elena and Nico outside. A sleek black sedan came to a stop near the fountain, and Pietro Romano stepped out, his expression unreadable.

"I've been thinking about our last conversation," he said, approaching them. "About Giulia, Angelo, and what you've uncovered. There's something you need to see."

Elena exchanged a curious glance with Nico. "What is it?"

Pietro gestured toward the car. "It's in my family archives. I thought it was just old papers, but after hearing what you've found, I think it might be important."

The Romano Archives

The Romano family's estate was smaller than the villa but carried a similar sense of history. Pietro led them to a private study, where a large chest sat in the center of the room. He opened it carefully, revealing stacks of papers, photographs, and personal effects.

"These belonged to Angelo," Pietro explained. "I've never gone through all of it, but there are letters, journals—things he never shared with anyone."

Elena's hands trembled as she reached for a bundle of letters tied with a faded ribbon. The handwriting was Angelo's, the ink still bold despite the years.

Giulia,

I don't know if I'll ever understand your choices, but I can't ignore what you've done for us. For me. You've given everything to protect us, even when I doubted you. I don't know if I can ever forgive myself for that. If we make it through this, I hope we can start again.

Tears blurred Elena's vision as she read the letter aloud. "He knew," she said softly. "He realized what she had done."

Pietro nodded, his expression solemn. "He never spoke of it, but I think it haunted him—how much he owed her, and how much he had doubted her."

Elena carefully placed the letter back in the chest. "This changes everything. Giulia wasn't just a misunderstood hero—she was the heart of the resistance."

"And Angelo's," Nico added quietly.

A New Perspective

Back at the villa, Elena and Nico worked late into the night, integrating the new discoveries into her growing manuscript. The villa's whispers felt louder now, their urgency pushing her forward.

Elena wrote of Angelo's doubts and Giulia's unwavering courage, of Livia's quiet strength and the resistance's reliance on the villa. Each story became a thread in a tapestry that stretched across generations, tying the past to the present.

As the stars appeared above the cypress trees, Nico placed a hand on her shoulder. "You've done something incredible," he said. "You've given these people their voices back."

Elena smiled faintly, her chest full. "And there's still more to tell."

Carrying the Legacy

The next morning, Elena stood in the courtyard, the manuscript tucked under her arm. The villa seemed to hum with approval, its presence steady and comforting.

Nico joined her, his expression filled with quiet pride. "What's next?"

Elena looked out at the horizon, her heart light despite the weight of the past. "We keep going. There's always another story waiting to be told."

As the sun rose higher, casting warm light over the villa's stones, Elena felt a sense of peace settle over her. The villa had held its secrets for decades, waiting for someone to uncover them. And now, as its stories unfolded beneath the cypress sky, she knew she was exactly where she was meant to be.

Chapter 24: Whispers of the Villa

The villa was quiet in the early morning light, its stones glowing softly under the rising sun. Elena stood on the balcony, overlooking the cliffs where the waves crashed against the rocks below. The manuscript sat on the table beside her, its pages filled with the stories she had uncovered. Yet, as she gazed at the horizon, she felt a familiar pull—the sense that the villa wasn't done speaking to her.

Nico appeared in the doorway, a mug of coffee in his hand. "You're up early."

Elena smiled faintly, her gaze still fixed on the sea. "I couldn't sleep. It feels like there's still something I'm missing."

Nico stepped onto the balcony, leaning against the railing. "You've uncovered so much already. What makes you think there's more?"

She turned to him, her expression thoughtful. "Because the villa feels different now. Quieter, but not finished. Like it still has something to tell me."

A Forgotten Key

Later that morning, as they organized the papers and artifacts in the library, a small envelope fell from one of Angelo's journals. Elena picked it up carefully, her fingers brushing the faded seal. Inside was a rusted key, its design intricate and unfamiliar.

"What's this?" Nico asked, leaning closer.

Elena turned the key over in her hands, her brow furrowing. "I don't know. It must have been hidden in the journal for a reason."

They examined the key closely, noting the faint markings etched into the metal. "It looks old," Nico said. "But it's not from the villa. None of the locks here use keys like this."

Elena's mind raced as she considered the possibilities. "If it's not for the villa, then maybe it's for something nearby. Angelo must have kept it for a reason."

A New Trail

Their search led them to the attic, where they sifted through trunks and crates in search of clues. Among the dusty belongings, Elena uncovered a map folded inside a leather case. The edges were brittle, but the markings were clear: a small clearing in the woods just beyond the villa was circled in ink.

"This must be it," Elena said, her pulse quickening. "The key must unlock something in the clearing."

Nico studied the map, his expression intrigued. "Let's find out."

The Clearing

The woods beyond the villa were dense, the air cool and filled with the scent of pine and earth. Elena and Nico followed the map's markings, their footsteps crunching softly on the forest floor. After some time, they arrived at the clearing, where a small stone structure stood partially hidden by overgrown vines.

The structure was modest, its entrance sealed by a heavy iron door. The keyhole matched the design of Angelo's key perfectly.

Elena's hands trembled as she inserted the key and turned it. The lock clicked, the sound echoing faintly in the still air. Together, they pushed the door open, revealing a narrow staircase that descended into darkness.

"Do you think it's safe?" Nico asked.

Elena nodded, her determination outweighing her fear. "We have to know."

A Hidden Chamber

The staircase led to a small underground chamber, its walls lined with shelves. Candles sat in sconces on the walls, their wax long since hardened. The air was damp and cool, carrying the faint scent of earth and age.

On the shelves were boxes filled with papers, books, and artifacts. At the center of the room stood a table, its surface covered with maps and letters. Elena's breath caught as she recognized the handwriting on one of the letters—it was Angelo's.

She picked up the letter carefully, her heart pounding as she read:

To those who come after me,

This place was a sanctuary during the darkest days. Here, we planned, we hoped, and we fought for a better future. If you have found this, it means the villa has chosen you to carry these stories forward. Remember us—not just for our sacrifices, but for our dreams. Let our voices live on through you.

Tears filled Elena's eyes as she finished reading. "He left this for someone like us," she whispered. "He knew the villa would protect these stories until the right time."

Nico placed a hand on her shoulder, his touch steady. "And now it's your turn to carry them forward."

The Legacy Grows

They spent hours in the chamber, cataloging its contents and piecing together the fragments of the resistance's history. Each artifact felt like a thread connecting the past to the present, weaving a story of resilience and hope.

Among the papers, Elena found another letter—this one written by Livia.

Angelo believed in this villa. He believed it would keep us safe, even when the world was falling apart. Now, it is our turn to protect it. This place holds more than just our memories—it holds our dreams, our love, and our hope for the future. To whoever finds this, thank you for listening to the whispers of these walls. May you carry our stories with pride.

Elena folded the letter carefully, her chest swelling with emotion. The villa's whispers seemed louder now, their urgency replaced by gratitude.

"They were waiting for someone to find this," she said. "To tell their story."

"And you've done that," Nico said. "But it's more than just their story now—it's yours, too."

A Night of Reflection

That night, back at the villa, Elena sat on the balcony overlooking the cliffs. The brooch and the letters rested on the table beside her, their weight both grounding and inspiring. The stars stretched endlessly above, their light mirrored in the dark waves below.

Nico joined her, carrying two glasses of wine. "To Angelo, Giulia, Livia, and everyone else who made this place what it is," he said, raising his glass.

Elena smiled, clinking her glass against his. "And to the villa—for keeping their voices alive."

As the cypress trees swayed gently in the breeze, Elena felt a quiet peace settle over her. The villa had revealed so much, its secrets no longer a burden but a gift. Beneath the cypress sky, she felt the weight of its legacy—and the hope it carried—rest lightly on her shoulders.

The story was far from over, but for the first time, she felt ready for whatever came next.

Chapter 25: A Tapestry of Memories

The villa seemed to hum with life in the days that followed the discovery of the hidden chamber. Elena worked tirelessly in the library, her desk covered with pages of notes, photographs, and letters. The voices of the past echoed through the villa's halls, no longer whispers but clear calls urging her to tell their stories.

Nico stood in the doorway, watching her with a mix of admiration and concern. "You've been at this for hours," he said. "Have you eaten anything today?"

Elena looked up from her notes, her hair falling loose from its tie. "Not yet. I can't stop. Every time I read something new, it feels like another piece of the puzzle falls into place."

He stepped into the room, setting a plate of bread and cheese beside her. "Even puzzles need breaks," he said, his voice gentle.

Elena smiled faintly, reaching for a piece of bread. "I'm close, Nico. I can feel it. The villa... it's almost like it's alive, guiding me."

Connecting the Threads

As she pieced together the artifacts from the chamber, Elena noticed a recurring motif: a cypress tree etched into the corners of maps, embossed on seals, and scrawled in the margins of letters. The symbol seemed to tie every fragment of the resistance's history to the villa itself.

"Look at this," she said, showing Nico a map with the cypress symbol drawn near Castelmare. "This tree—it's everywhere. It must have meant something to them."

Nico studied the map, his brow furrowed. "The cypress tree has always been a symbol of resilience. It could be their way of marking a safe place, or a sign of hope."

Elena nodded, her mind racing. "The villa is surrounded by cypress trees. Maybe it wasn't just a home—it was their sanctuary, their symbol of everything they were fighting for."

She flipped through one of Angelo's journals, her heart pounding as she found a passage that seemed to confirm her theory.

April 1944

The cypress trees stand tall, even as the world burns around them. They remind me of what we are fighting for—strength, endurance, hope. This villa, these trees, they are our refuge. Our promise that even in the darkest times, something can survive.

Elena's voice trembled as she read the words aloud. "He saw the villa as more than just a place. It was their symbol of survival."

A Gathering of Stories

With the puzzle coming into focus, Elena and Nico decided to organize a gathering at the villa. They invited the people of Castelmare, including those whose families had ties to the resistance. The goal was simple: to share what they had uncovered and invite others to contribute their own stories.

The courtyard buzzed with activity as neighbors arrived, bringing photographs, letters, and personal accounts. Pietro Romano stood near the fountain, holding a framed photograph of Angelo. Marcello Bonetti shared tales of daring missions, his voice steady with pride.

Elena moved through the crowd, her notebook in hand, recording each story and collecting every fragment of memory. Each voice added depth to the tapestry she was weaving, turning the villa into a living archive of resilience and love.

A Surprising Revelation

As the evening unfolded, an elderly woman approached Elena, her cane tapping softly against the stone floor. Her dark eyes were sharp, her expression thoughtful.

"You must be the one who has been uncovering the villa's secrets," she said, her voice steady despite her years.

Elena smiled warmly. "I'm trying. Do you have a story to share?"

The woman nodded. "My name is Bianca Ferrante. My mother, Lucia, was part of the resistance. She worked closely with Angelo and Giulia."

Elena's breath caught. "Lucia Ferrante? She's mentioned in some of the records we found."

Bianca's gaze softened. "My mother rarely spoke of those days, but she always told me one thing: Giulia Orlandi was the bravest woman she ever knew. She saved my mother's life during the war."

"What happened?" Elena asked, her voice trembling.

Bianca leaned on her cane, her expression distant. "There was an ambush. The enemy had discovered one of their safe houses. Giulia stayed behind to lead them away, giving my mother and the others time to escape. She nearly didn't make it out, but she did. And she never asked for thanks."

Tears welled in Elena's eyes as she listened. "She gave everything for the people she loved."

Bianca nodded. "And she never asked for recognition. But she deserves it now."

Carrying the Legacy

As the gathering came to an end, Elena stood beneath the cypress trees, the stars glittering above her. The villa seemed alive with the stories it had held for so long, its presence a steady companion.

Nico joined her, his expression filled with quiet pride. "You've done something incredible tonight," he said. "You've given these stories a voice."

Elena looked at him, her chest tight with emotion. "It's not just me. It's the villa—it's everyone who's shared their memories. Together, we've brought the past to life."

He reached for her hand, his touch warm and grounding. "And now, what's next?"

Elena glanced at the villa, its stones glowing softly in the moonlight. "I finish the story. And I make sure it's one they'll never forget."

As the night deepened, Elena felt a quiet peace settle over her. The villa had given her a purpose, a connection to the past that anchored her in the present. Beneath the cypress sky, she knew she was part of something greater—a tapestry of love, resilience, and hope that would endure for generations to come.

Chapter 26: Voices in the Walls

The villa was silent as the early morning light spilled through the arched windows, casting golden beams across the library. Elena sat at her desk, surrounded by the remnants of the previous evening's gathering—notes scribbled in her notebook, photographs loaned by neighbors, and fragments of stories that had added new layers to her manuscript.

The quiet hum of the villa seemed louder today, its presence a steady reminder of the stories it had safeguarded for so long. She rested her hand on the brooch, the cool metal grounding her as she reflected on the weight of her discoveries.

Nico entered, carrying a tray with coffee and pastries. "You didn't sleep much," he observed, setting the tray down beside her.

Elena smiled faintly. "There's too much to process. Every story I heard last night—it's like the villa keeps pulling me deeper."

Nico sat across from her, his gaze steady. "Maybe that's what it's meant to do. To guide you to the truth."

A Fragmented Puzzle

As Elena sifted through the new stories and artifacts, a pattern began to emerge. Each fragment—every letter, every photograph—seemed to connect to a central theme: the villa as a haven for resilience and hope.

She paused on a photograph Bianca Ferrante had given her. It showed a group of resistance members gathered near the villa's fountain. Giulia stood in the center, her expression strong but tinged with exhaustion. Angelo was off to the side, his posture rigid, his gaze distant.

"This was taken just weeks before the ambush Bianca described," Elena murmured. "They look so... fragile. As if they knew what was coming."

Nico leaned over, studying the photograph. "And yet, they kept going. Because they believed in something bigger than themselves."

Elena nodded, her chest tightening. "I need to understand what drove them. What gave them the strength to keep fighting."

A Forgotten Letter

As she organized the papers from the gathering, Elena found a small envelope tucked inside one of the stacks. The paper was yellowed, the handwriting unfamiliar. She opened it carefully, her heart racing as she read the words.

To Giulia,

I have doubted you more times than I care to admit, but I see now that my doubts were a reflection of my own fears, not your actions. You have been our anchor, our light in the darkness. Whatever happens, I want you to know that I trust you—and that I am sorry for ever questioning your loyalty.

Angelo

Elena's breath caught as she read the final line. "He did trust her," she said softly. "In the end, he knew the truth."

Nico's expression softened as he took the letter. "But did she ever know that? Or did she carry his doubts to the grave?"

The question hung heavily in the air, the weight of it pressing against Elena's chest. "I need to find out," she said, her voice trembling. "If Angelo's faith came too late, then that's part of their story, too."

A Visit to the Past

Elena and Nico decided to visit Pietro Romano again, hoping he might have insight into Angelo's final days. The drive to the Romano estate was quiet, the rolling hills bathed in soft sunlight.

Pietro greeted them warmly, his curiosity piqued as they showed him the letter. He studied it carefully, his brow furrowing. "This must have been written near the end of the war," he said. "My grandfather rarely spoke of that time, but I know he carried regrets with him—regrets about Giulia."

Elena leaned forward, her pulse quickening. "Did he ever say if he told her? If she knew he trusted her?"

Pietro shook his head slowly. "I don't think so. Angelo wasn't good at expressing himself, especially when it came to emotions. But I believe he wanted to make things right."

Elena's heart sank. "So she never knew."

Pietro's expression softened. "She may not have needed to hear it. Giulia knew who she was and what she stood for. That was enough for her."

An Unlikely Discovery

Back at the villa, Elena retreated to the library, her thoughts heavy. As she sifted through the papers on her desk, a scrap of paper fell to the floor. It was a fragment of Livia's journal, one she hadn't noticed before.

May 1944

Angelo spoke of Giulia today. He seemed restless, his guilt spilling into every word. I told him that forgiveness is not always about being heard—it's about finding peace within ourselves. I hope he finds it someday.

Elena's breath caught as she read the words. "Livia knew," she said softly. "She knew what he carried, and she tried to help him let it go."

Nico rested a hand on her shoulder. "And maybe that's why she wrote the letter we found in the church. She wanted to leave that peace behind for someone like you to find."

Elena nodded, her resolve hardening. "Then I need to honor her. To honor all of them."

Carrying the Voices Forward

That evening, Elena sat on the balcony, the brooch glinting softly in the moonlight. The stars stretched endlessly above her, their light mirrored in the dark waves below. She picked up her pen, her heart full as she began to write.

They were flawed, as all people are. They carried doubts and fears, made mistakes and misjudgments. But they also carried love, hope, and an unyielding belief in something greater than themselves. This is their story—not just of what they lost, but of what they left behind.

The words flowed easily now, each one carrying the weight of the villa's legacy. Elena wrote late into the night, her connection to the past grounding her in the present.

As the cypress trees swayed gently in the breeze, Elena felt a quiet peace settle over her. The villa's whispers seemed softer now, their urgency replaced by gratitude. The story was no longer just about Angelo, Giulia, or Livia—it was about all of them, and the resilience that bound them together.

Beneath the cypress sky, Elena knew she was exactly where she was meant to be.

Chapter 27: The Shadows of Forgiveness

The morning sun cast long shadows across the villa's courtyard, illuminating the cypress trees that swayed gently in the breeze. Elena stood near the fountain, the letter from Angelo in her hand. The words carried the weight of unspoken apologies, the regret of someone who had doubted too late. She traced her fingers along the edge of the paper, her thoughts a tangle of questions.

"Do you think she forgave him?" she asked, her voice barely above a whisper.

Nico stood beside her, his arms crossed as he studied the letter. "Giulia wasn't the type to hold grudges," he said. "From everything we've learned, she was focused on the bigger picture. I think she would have understood."

Elena looked up at the cypress trees, their branches stretching toward the sky. "It just feels so... unfinished. Angelo carried guilt, Giulia carried doubt, and Livia carried their secrets. It's like none of them truly got to let go."

"Maybe that's why the villa kept their stories alive," Nico said. "So someone like you could give them the closure they couldn't find."

A Return to the Clearing

Later that morning, Elena and Nico returned to the hidden chamber in the woods. The air was cool and still, the stone structure covered in shadows cast by the surrounding trees.

Elena carried a small notebook, determined to document every detail of the chamber and its contents.

As they descended the narrow staircase, the damp air seemed to close around them, the scent of earth and age thick in the space. The room was just as they had left it, its shelves lined with boxes and papers, the table still covered with maps and letters.

Elena moved to the table, her fingers brushing across the surface as if seeking something invisible. She paused at a small, folded piece of paper tucked beneath a stack of maps. It wasn't as faded as the other documents, its ink still bold.

"What is it?" Nico asked, stepping closer.

Elena unfolded the paper carefully, her heart pounding as she recognized the handwriting—it was Giulia's.

To Angelo,

If I never get the chance to say this, let me say it here. I never hated you for doubting me. I understood your fear, your need to protect the resistance. But I want you to know that I forgave you long before you ever needed forgiveness. I loved you, Angelo, not for your trust but for your heart. Carry that with you, always.

Giulia

Tears blurred Elena's vision as she read the letter aloud. "She forgave him," she said softly. "She never stopped believing in him, even when he doubted her."

Nico rested a hand on her shoulder, his voice steady. "And now you've found the piece that Angelo never could. Maybe that's the closure they both needed."

A New Chapter

That evening, back at the villa, Elena sat at her desk with the letters spread before her. Angelo's regret, Giulia's forgiveness, and Livia's quiet strength formed a tapestry of resilience and love that spanned decades. The villa seemed to hum with approval, its presence comforting and grounding.

Elena picked up her pen, the words flowing easily as she began to write:

The villa held their secrets, but it also held their truths. It was here that they loved, fought, doubted, and forgave. And though their lives were marked by loss, they were also defined by courage. This is not just their story—it is a story of hope, of resilience, and of the power of love to endure.

The words felt right, each one a step closer to honoring the people who had called the villa home.

A Night of Reflection

Later that night, Elena and Nico sat on the balcony, the stars stretching endlessly above them. The air was cool, carrying the faint scent of jasmine and salt from the sea. Elena held Giulia's letter in her hands, its weight both heavy and freeing.

"She forgave him," she said again, her voice filled with quiet wonder. "She didn't need his apology to find peace."

Nico nodded. "Because she knew who she was. She didn't need validation—she just needed to know she had done what was right."

Elena looked at him, her heart swelling with gratitude. "Thank you," she said softly. "For being here, for helping me see this through."

Nico smiled, his eyes warm. "I'm not going anywhere."

As the cypress trees swayed gently in the breeze, Elena felt a quiet peace settle over her. The villa had given her so much—answers, purpose, and a connection to a legacy that would endure. Beneath the cypress sky, she knew the story wasn't just about the past—it was about carrying that hope into the future.

Chapter 28: A Place for Redemption

The morning light streamed through the windows of the villa, casting a golden glow on the library walls. Elena sat at her desk, her fingers running over the edges of Giulia's letter. The villa's quiet hum seemed more pronounced today, as if it was urging her toward the next step.

"This isn't just about telling their story anymore," she said aloud, her voice steady. "It's about giving them the redemption they never had."

Nico, seated nearby with a cup of coffee, looked up from the notebook he was reviewing. "What do you mean?"

Elena set the letter down and leaned back in her chair. "Giulia forgave Angelo, but he never forgave himself. Livia carried their secrets, but no one ever truly understood her strength. And the resistance... so many of them have been forgotten."

"And you want to change that," Nico said, his voice full of quiet admiration.

Elena nodded, her resolve firm. "I want to create a space where their stories can live—not just on paper, but here, in the villa."

A Vision for the Villa

Later that morning, Elena walked the grounds of the villa, her notebook in hand. The cypress trees swayed gently in the breeze, their presence a constant reminder of the strength and resilience the villa symbolized. She paused in the courtyard, her gaze sweeping over the fountain and the weathered stones.

"What if the villa became a place for memory?" she said, turning to Nico, who had followed her outside. "A museum, or a center for history and storytelling. A place where people can come to learn about the resistance, about the sacrifices made here."

Nico tilted his head, considering her words. "It could work. The villa already carries so much history—it's practically alive with it. But it would be a big project."

Elena smiled, a spark of excitement lighting her eyes. "It's worth it. If we can bring these stories to life, we can honor everyone who fought and loved here."

A Plan in Motion

The following days were a whirlwind of activity. Elena reached out to local historians, archivists, and neighbors who had shared their stories at the gathering. Pietro Romano offered his family's archives, and Marcello Bonetti volunteered to help curate exhibits.

The villa buzzed with energy as Elena and Nico began transforming its rooms into spaces dedicated to the past. The library became a research hub, its shelves filled with letters, journals, and photographs. The great hall was cleared to display artifacts, including resistance maps, Giulia's brooch, and Angelo's letters.

"We'll need to add plaques and descriptions," Elena said, jotting notes in her notebook. "And we should create a timeline—something that ties all the stories together."

"And what about the cypress trees?" Nico asked, gesturing to the grove that surrounded the villa.

Elena smiled. "They'll be our symbol. Just like they were for Angelo and Giulia."

An Unexpected Gift

One afternoon, as they worked in the library, a knock at the door interrupted their progress. Elena opened it to find Bianca Ferrante standing on the threshold, holding a small wooden box.

"I thought you might like this," Bianca said, her voice soft. "It belonged to my mother. She always said it should return to the villa one day."

Elena accepted the box carefully, her heart racing. Inside was a delicate silver necklace, its pendant shaped like a cypress tree. Alongside it was a small journal filled with Lucia's handwritten notes.

"She kept this during the war," Bianca explained. "It's full of her thoughts, her fears, and her hopes for the future. I think it belongs here."

Tears welled in Elena's eyes as she hugged Bianca. "Thank you," she said. "This means more than I can say."

The Villa's Transformation

As the weeks passed, the villa began to take on a new life. The stories of Angelo, Giulia, Livia, and the resistance filled its halls, their voices brought to life through exhibits and displays. Visitors began arriving, drawn by the villa's history and the powerful legacy it represented.

Elena stood in the courtyard one evening, watching as the last of the day's visitors left. The cypress trees swayed gently above, their whispers carrying a sense of completion.

"You did it," Nico said, joining her. "The villa is alive again."

Elena smiled, her chest swelling with pride and gratitude. "We did it. And it's just the beginning."

A Night of Celebration

That night, the villa hosted a celebration to mark its transformation. Neighbors and supporters filled the courtyard, their laughter and conversation mingling with the soft music that played in the background. Pietro gave a heartfelt speech about his grandfather's courage, while Marcello shared stories of Giulia's daring missions.

Elena stood near the fountain, a glass of wine in her hand, as Nico approached. "To the villa," he said, raising his glass.

"To the villa," Elena echoed, her voice filled with emotion.

As the stars stretched across the night sky, the villa seemed to hum with approval. It was no longer just a home—it was a living testament to love, resilience, and hope. Beneath the cypress sky, Elena felt a quiet peace settle over her.

The past had found its voice, and the villa's story was far from over

Chapter 29: The Villa's Heart

The villa was quiet the next morning, its halls basking in the soft glow of the rising sun. Elena walked through the great hall, now transformed into an exhibit space. The artifacts of the resistance stood proudly in glass cases: Giulia's brooch, Angelo's letters, the maps that had once guided their every move. Visitors would soon arrive, but for now, the villa was hers.

She paused by a display dedicated to Livia, where her journal lay open to a passage about the villa's role during the war. Livia's words spoke of courage, of resilience, and of a hope that had carried them through the darkest times.

"You've given her voice back," Nico said from behind her, his tone quiet but filled with admiration.

Elena turned to him, her expression thoughtful. "I think the villa gave her voice back. It was here all along—I just had to listen."

A Surprise Visitor

Later that morning, as visitors began to arrive, a familiar face appeared among the crowd. Bianca Ferrante walked through the courtyard, her steps steady despite her age. She carried a small bouquet of wildflowers, her eyes scanning the villa with a mix of curiosity and reverence.

Elena greeted her warmly. "Bianca, it's so good to see you."

Bianca smiled, holding out the flowers. "These are for the villa. My mother always said wildflowers belonged here, as a reminder of its strength."

Elena accepted the bouquet, her heart swelling. "Thank you. That's beautiful."

Bianca glanced around, her gaze lingering on the cypress trees. "This place—it's more than just a building. It feels alive, doesn't it?"

Elena nodded, her voice soft. "It does. And it's because of people like your mother, like Giulia and Angelo, who gave it life."

Rekindling Connections

As the day unfolded, visitors moved through the villa, their voices low as they read the plaques and studied the exhibits. Elena watched as two young women paused in front of a photograph of the resistance members. They whispered to each other, pointing at the names.

One of the women turned to Elena. "Were these people all part of the resistance?"

"Yes," Elena replied. "They fought to protect Castelmare and its people. Each of them played a role, whether in the shadows or on the front lines."

The women exchanged glances, their expressions thoughtful. "It's incredible," one of them said. "To think that they did so much, and yet so many of their stories were almost lost."

Elena smiled, her chest tight with pride. "That's why we're here—to make sure they're never forgotten."

A Personal Reflection

That evening, after the last visitor had left, Elena stood in the courtyard beneath the cypress trees. The stars glittered above, their light soft and steady. Nico joined her, his presence as grounding as always.

"You've created something incredible," he said, his voice filled with quiet admiration. "The villa—it's alive again because of you."

Elena shook her head. "It's alive because of everyone who shared their stories, everyone who fought to protect it. I just gave it a way to speak."

Nico smiled, his gaze steady. "And you've done it beautifully."

Elena looked out at the trees, their branches swaying gently in the breeze. "The villa still has more to say, though. I can feel it. There are stories we haven't uncovered yet."

"Then we'll keep looking," Nico said. "Together."

A Legacy Fulfilled

As the night deepened, Elena felt a quiet peace settle over her. The villa had become more than just a home or a museum—it was a living testament to the resilience and love that had defined its history. Beneath the cypress sky, it stood as a beacon of hope, its whispers carrying the stories of the past into the future.

And as Elena stood there, her hand in Nico's, she knew that her work wasn't finished. The villa's story was still unfolding, and she was ready to see where it would lead next.

Chapter 30: The Cypress Grove

The morning mist clung to the cypress trees as Elena stepped into the grove behind the villa. The air was cool and fragrant, filled with the earthy scent of the forest. She carried a notebook under her arm, determined to capture the last pieces of the villa's story. This grove, she realized, had been a silent witness to so much—conversations, plans, betrayals, and promises.

Nico followed a few steps behind, his steady presence comforting. "What are we looking for this time?" he asked.

"Answers," Elena replied, her voice thoughtful. "I feel like there's something we've missed. The villa has given us so much, but I can't shake the feeling that the grove holds something important."

They walked in silence, their footsteps soft against the forest floor. The grove seemed to hum with life, its shadows shifting as the sun began to rise higher in the sky.

A Hidden Marker

Elena paused near a clearing, her gaze drawn to an unusual arrangement of stones at the base of one of the largest cypress trees. The stones were smooth and worn, their placement too deliberate to be natural.

"Here," she said, crouching down to examine them. "This isn't random."

Nico knelt beside her, brushing away the dirt that had settled over the stones. "It looks like some kind of marker."

As they cleared the area, they uncovered a small, rusted plaque embedded in the ground. The words were faint but still legible: In memory of those who gave everything beneath these trees.

Elena's breath caught. "It's a memorial," she whispered. "They must have created this after the war—for the resistance."

Nico ran his fingers over the plaque, his expression somber. "It's been forgotten, just like so many of their stories."

Elena stood, her chest tightening with resolve. "Not anymore. We'll restore it. This grove—it's part of the villa's legacy. People should know what happened here."

Restoring the Grove

Over the following days, the grove became the focus of their efforts. With help from Pietro, Marcello, and the community, they began clearing the area, uncovering more markers that had been hidden by time. Each one bore the name of a resistance member who had fought to protect Castelmare.

As the grove was restored, it transformed into a tranquil space filled with history and remembrance. Benches were added beneath the trees, and paths were cleared to allow visitors to walk among the markers. The cypress trees stood tall, their presence a testament to the strength and endurance of those they honored.

A Dedication Ceremony

On the day of the grove's dedication, the villa was alive with activity. Neighbors and visitors gathered in the courtyard, their voices low with reverence. Elena stood at the front of the group, her notebook in hand.

"This grove has always been a part of the villa," she began, her voice steady despite the emotions swirling within her. "It was here that plans were made, sacrifices were endured, and hope was kept alive. Today, we honor those who gave everything beneath these trees—their courage, their resilience, and their love."

As she spoke, she felt the presence of the villa around her, its whispers now a steady hum of approval. The grove, once forgotten, was now a place of memory and connection, a bridge between the past and the present.

Pietro stepped forward, holding a bouquet of wildflowers. "For Angelo," he said softly, placing the flowers at the base of one of the markers.

Others followed, leaving flowers, letters, and tokens of remembrance. The grove became a tapestry of love and gratitude, its beauty a reflection of the lives it honored.

A Quiet Moment

That evening, after the visitors had gone, Elena and Nico returned to the grove. The air was cool, the stars bright against the night sky. The cypress trees swayed gently, their whispers carrying the weight of generations.

"You've done it," Nico said, his voice soft. "You've brought their stories to life."

Elena smiled, her chest swelling with gratitude. "We did it. The villa, the grove—it's all part of something bigger than us."

As they stood beneath the trees, the villa's presence wrapped around them like an embrace. Its stories were no longer hidden, its whispers no longer urgent. The cypress grove was alive again, a sanctuary for memory, love, and hope.

And as Elena looked up at the stars, she knew that the villa's legacy would endure—its heart carried forward by those who had listened, loved, and believed. Beneath the cypress sky, the story was still unfolding, and she was ready to see where it would lead next.

Chapter 31: Threads of the Future

The morning air was crisp and filled with the soft rustle of leaves as Elena walked through the restored cypress grove. The markers glinted in the sunlight, their inscriptions now clear and enduring. Each name was a story reclaimed, a voice given back to history. The grove felt alive, not just as a memorial but as a promise to remember.

Nico appeared at her side, his hands tucked into his pockets. "The dedication yesterday was incredible," he said. "I saw people crying, Elena. You've given them something they didn't even know they needed."

Elena smiled softly, her gaze sweeping the grove. "It's not just me. It's the villa, the community, the stories that refused to be forgotten. This place—it's a part of all of us now."

Nico tilted his head, studying her. "And what about you? What's next for Elena Marconi?"

An Unexpected Opportunity

Later that day, as Elena worked in the library, she received an email from a prestigious historical organization. They had heard about the villa's transformation and the work she had done to uncover the stories of the resistance. The email invited her to present her findings at an upcoming conference on wartime history.

Elena read the email twice, her heart racing. The thought of sharing the villa's story on such a large platform was exhilarating—and terrifying.

Nico walked in, noticing her expression. "What's wrong?" he asked, setting a cup of tea on the desk.

"Nothing," Elena replied, handing him her phone. "Or maybe everything."

He read the email, his eyes widening. "Elena, this is incredible. They want you to speak at a major conference."

She nodded, her fingers twisting the edge of her notebook. "I'm just not sure I'm ready. What if I can't do justice to their stories?"

Nico crouched beside her, his gaze steady. "You've already done justice to their stories. That's why they want you to speak. You don't have to be perfect—you just have to be you."

Preparing the Story

Over the next few weeks, Elena poured herself into preparing for the conference. She carefully selected artifacts, photographs, and excerpts from journals to include in her presentation. Each detail was chosen with care, every word crafted to honor the people whose lives had shaped the villa.

The library became a hive of activity as neighbors and historians came to help. Marcello shared his memories of Giulia, while Pietro loaned family heirlooms to include in the display. Even Bianca Ferrante brought a letter from her mother, its words a testament to the resilience of the resistance.

One evening, as she rehearsed her speech in the courtyard, Nico sat nearby, his expression encouraging. "You're ready," he said after she finished. "This is exactly what the world needs to hear."

Elena exhaled deeply, her nerves easing under his steady gaze. "I hope so. It's not just about the past—it's about what we can learn from it."

The Presentation

The day of the conference arrived, and the grand hall buzzed with anticipation. Elena stood backstage, her heart pounding as she adjusted the microphone on her lapel. The artifacts from the villa were displayed on a table nearby, each one a piece of the puzzle she had worked so hard to uncover.

When her name was announced, the audience erupted in applause. Elena stepped onto the stage, the weight of the villa's stories pressing against her chest like a comforting hand. She began to speak, her voice steady and clear.

"This is a story about a villa—a place that held not just people, but secrets, love, and resilience. It is also a story about the people who called it home, who fought for something greater than themselves, and who left behind a legacy that still whispers to us today."

As she spoke, she saw the audience lean forward, captivated by her words. She shared Giulia's bravery, Angelo's redemption, and Livia's quiet strength. She described the cypress grove, the markers, and the way the villa had transformed into a living testament to hope.

When she finished, the room erupted in a standing ovation. Elena blinked back tears, her heart full. She had done it—not just for herself, but for the villa and the people it had sheltered.

A New Beginning

Back at the villa, Elena stood in the courtyard, the stars glittering above. The conference had been a success, and the villa was now gaining recognition as a historical landmark. Visitors arrived daily, eager to walk through its halls and learn its stories.

Nico joined her, his expression warm. "You've done something amazing, Elena. You've given the past a voice—and a future."

She looked at him, her chest swelling with gratitude. "And I couldn't have done it without you."

As they stood beneath the cypress trees, Elena felt a quiet peace settle over her. The villa's whispers were no longer urgent; they were steady and content. Its stories had been heard, its legacy carried forward.

And as Elena looked out at the grove, she knew her journey wasn't over. Beneath the cypress sky, the future was waiting, and she was ready to embrace it.

Chapter 32: A Future Among the Cypress

The villa seemed to glow in the soft light of dawn. Elena stood on the balcony, watching the cypress trees sway gently in the breeze. Below, the courtyard was quiet, still carrying the echoes of the conference and the many visitors who had come to honor the villa's history. For the first time in months, she felt at peace.

Nico appeared behind her, carrying a cup of coffee. "You're up early," he said, offering her the mug.

Elena smiled as she took it. "Couldn't sleep. I've been thinking about what's next."

He leaned against the railing, his gaze thoughtful. "You've done so much already. The villa's alive again—it's a place where people can connect with the past. What more could there be?"

Elena's smile widened as she looked at him. "That's just it. This isn't the end—it's the beginning. There's so much more we can do."

A Legacy of Learning

Elena spent the next few days brainstorming ideas for the villa's future. She envisioned it not just as a historical site, but as a center for learning and inspiration. Classes on local history, workshops on storytelling, and events to honor the resilience of those who had come before.

"We could host programs for students," she told Nico one evening as they sat in the library. "Imagine young people coming here, walking through the grove, and learning about the resistance—not just as names on a plaque, but as real people who made real sacrifices."

Nico nodded, his expression encouraging. "And you could lead the programs. You've brought these stories to life in a way that no one else could."

Elena hesitated, her heart racing at the thought. "I'm not a teacher."

"No," Nico said with a smile. "You're a storyteller. And that's exactly what they need."

A Community Effort

As word spread about Elena's vision, the community rallied around her. Marcello offered to lead guided tours of the grove, sharing his firsthand accounts of the resistance. Pietro proposed a partnership with local schools to bring students to the villa. Even Bianca Ferrante contributed, volunteering to host storytelling sessions about her mother's life.

The villa became a hub of activity, its halls filled with the voices of children, families, and scholars. Each person who visited left with a deeper connection to the past and a renewed sense of hope for the future.

One afternoon, as Elena walked through the grove, she spotted a group of students sitting beneath the cypress trees, their teacher reading from one of Angelo's letters. The sight filled her chest with pride and gratitude.

"This is what it's all about," she said softly.

Nico, who stood beside her, squeezed her hand. "You've built something incredible, Elena. The villa—it's become so much more than a memory."

A Personal Journey

Amid the flurry of activity, Elena began working on a book about the villa and the stories it had revealed. She poured her heart into every page, weaving together the lives of Angelo, Giulia, and Livia with the voices of the resistance and the community that had kept their memory alive.

One evening, as she sat in the library, Nico entered with a package in his hands. "This came for you," he said, setting it on the desk.

Elena opened it to find a letter from the publisher she had submitted her manuscript to. Her breath caught as she read the words: We are thrilled to offer you a contract for your book. It is a remarkable story, and we are honored to help you share it with the world.

She looked up at Nico, her eyes wide with disbelief. "They want to publish it."

His face broke into a grin as he pulled her into a hug. "Of course they do. It's amazing, Elena. You're amazing."

A Celebration of Love

The following weekend, the villa hosted a celebration to mark the publication of Elena's book. Friends, neighbors, and visitors gathered in the courtyard, their laughter and conversation mingling with the soft strains of music.

Elena stood near the fountain, a copy of her book in her hands. The cover featured the villa silhouetted against the cypress trees, the title bold and clear: Beneath the Cypress Sky: Stories of Love and Resilience.

Nico joined her, his expression filled with pride. "To the storyteller," he said, raising his glass.

"To the villa," Elena replied, her voice filled with emotion. "And to everyone who made it what it is."

As the night deepened and the stars filled the sky, Elena felt a sense of completion—but also of new beginnings. The villa's whispers were no longer urgent; they were a steady, comforting hum. Its stories had found their voice, and its legacy was secure.

And as Elena stood beneath the cypress trees, her hand in Nico's, she knew the story wasn't just about the past. It was about the future, the people who would come, and the love that would always endure beneath the cypress sky.

EPILOGUE: BENEATH THE Cypress Sky

Years passed, and the villa thrived. Its once-silent halls now echoed with laughter, conversations, and the footsteps of visitors from around the world. The cypress grove stood as a quiet sanctuary, its markers a testament to the lives it honored. The villa had become more than a historical site—it was a living legacy, a place where the past and present intertwined.

Elena sat on the balcony overlooking the grove, a warm breeze carrying the scent of jasmine and salt from the sea. The first edition of her book rested on the table beside her, its pages filled with the stories she had uncovered. The world had embraced the villa's history, and her work had sparked conversations about resilience, love, and the power of memory.

Nico stepped out onto the balcony, two mugs of coffee in hand. He set one beside her and took a seat, his gaze soft as he looked out at the grove. "It never gets old, does it?" he said.

Elena smiled, her heart light. "Never. The villa has a way of making everything feel timeless."

They sat in companionable silence, the cypress trees swaying gently in the breeze. Below, a group of visitors walked through the grove, pausing to read the markers and reflect on the lives they represented. A young girl ran ahead, her laughter ringing out as she pointed to the largest tree.

Elena watched the scene with quiet pride. The villa's stories were alive, carried forward by the people who came to listen and learn. Its whispers had become a chorus, woven into the fabric of the present.

A Legacy That Endures

As the sun dipped below the horizon, painting the sky in hues of gold and violet, Elena turned to Nico. "Do you think the villa will still stand a hundred years from now?"

He reached for her hand, his touch warm and reassuring. "Absolutely. It's more than just a place—it's a symbol. And symbols like this don't fade."

Elena squeezed his hand, her chest full. "I hope so. I want it to be a place where people can always come to remember, to feel connected to something bigger than themselves."

"And because of you," Nico said softly, "it will be."

As the stars began to appear, Elena leaned back, her heart full and her spirit at peace. Beneath the cypress sky, the villa's legacy would endure, carried forward by the love and resilience it had always embodied.

The past had found its voice, the present had embraced it, and the future would carry it onward. And in the quiet hum of the villa's whispers, Elena knew that she, too, had become a part of its story—a story that would live on, always, beneath the cypress sky.

Also by Kenneth Thomas

Alchemists Cost
Eternity's Past

Beneath Cypress Skies
Another Cypress Sky

Harrow Harbor Mysteries
Whispering Harbor Mystery
The Secret of the Cavern
The Ghost Ships Shadow

Moonlight Pact series
The Moonlight Pact
The Rift Redemption
The Riftbound Legacy

A Love Written In Starlight
The Twilight Alchemy of Jekyll and Hyde
Whispers of the Wild Frontier
The Last Prediction
Tales of the Midnight Traveler
Echoes of Eden
Throne of Light
The Alchemist's Cost
Ashes of Ambition